Perhaps he has a date.

Maura flushed at her presumptuousness. She should have called before showing up at his door.

"Well, I should be going," she said abruptly. She gave a short nod toward the casserole dish, avoiding his eyes. "The stew will keep, you know, if you've something else planned for the evening."

"But I don't have anything planned," Nate said.

She glanced up. "No?" She felt strangely relieved by his assertion.

"Not a thing." Again, he gestured to the chair in front of her in an invitation to sit. "In fact, if you don't have any other plans yourself, would you like to have supper with me?"

No, he didn't have a date, but he was making one right now.

He's looking for a wife....

Dear Reader,

Happy Valentine's Day! Love is in the air...and between every page of a Silhouette Romance novel. Treat yourself to six new stories guaranteed to remind you what Valentine's Day is all about....

In Liz Ireland's *The Birds and the Bees,* Kyle Weston could truly be a FABULOUS FATHER. That's why young Maggie Moore would do *anything* to reunite him with his past secret love—her mother, Mary.

You'll find romance and adventure in Joleen Daniels's latest book, *Jilted!* Kidnapped at the altar, Jenny Landon is forced to choose between the man she truly loves—and the man she *must* marry.

The legacy of SMYTHESHIRE, MASSACHUSETTS continues in Elizabeth August's *The Seeker.*

Don't miss the battle of wills when a fast-talking lawyer tries to woo a sweet-tongued rancher back to civilization in Stella Bagwell's *Corporate Cowgirl.* Jodi O'Donnell takes us back to the small-town setting of her first novel in *The Farmer Takes a Wife.* And you'll be SPELLBOUND by Pat Montana's handsome—and magical—hero in this talented author's first novel, *One Unbelievable Man.*

Happy reading!

Anne Canadeo
Senior Editor

Please address questions and book requests to:
Reader Service
U.S.: P.O. Box 1325, Buffalo, NY 14269
Canadian: P.O. Box 1050, Niagara Falls, Ont. L2E 7G7

THE FARMER
TAKES A WIFE
Jodi O'Donnell

Silhouette
ROMANCE™
Published by Silhouette Books
America's Publisher of Contemporary Romance

This one's just for Darrel:
Gotcha, didn't I?

ACKNOWLEDGMENTS
For information on the Master Gardener program, I thank my sister,
Jacqueline O'Donnell Mobley.
For information on libraries, Little League and lazy eye,
my thanks to Ann Watts, Ron Kamps and Vicki Lynn Leckey.
And special thanks to my mother, Jacqueline O'Donnell.

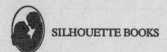 SILHOUETTE BOOKS

ISBN 0-373-08992-9

THE FARMER TAKES A WIFE

Books by Jodi O'Donnell

Silhouette Romance

Still Sweet on Him #969
The Farmer Takes a Wife #992

JODI O'DONNELL

considers herself living proof that "writing what you know" works. She grew up in Iowa but moved to California—only to marry the hometown boy she'd known since fifth grade. Her first novel, *Still Sweet on Him* won the Romance Writers of America 1992 Golden Heart Award for Best Unpublished Traditional Romance.

Jodi and her husband, Darrel, run a successful consulting business near Dallas, Texas, with the aid of their two computer cats, ASCII and ECCDIC.

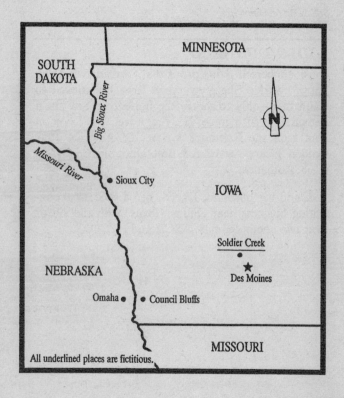

MINNESOTA

SOUTH DAKOTA

Big Sioux River

Missouri River

• Sioux City

IOWA

NEBRASKA

Soldier Creek
•
★
Des Moines

Omaha •   • Council Bluffs

All underlined places are fictitious.

MISSOURI

Chapter One

Maura Foster plunged her hands into the small section of moist Iowa soil she'd loosened with her trowel. Black as cinders, springy as rising bread dough, the loam clumped between her fingers and chilled her wrists in a sensation she'd long missed. She closed her eyes and sighed as if sinking into a warm bubble bath.

Maura chuckled. She always went a little crazy this time of year, but the fever was especially strong this spring, though with good reason. After two years of going without, she'd have a vegetable garden again. And flowers, more than just in window boxes or blooming in clay pots on a minuscule patio.

"This year," she told herself, "I'll have *flowers*—bleeding hearts, impatiens, columbine, bluebells, bachelor buttons, everything."

Oh, and snapdragons. Davey would want those in their new garden. She wondered if he'd outgrown the darling habit of calling them "snackdragons," as he'd done when he had been three.

Remember that, Wayne? You taught him how to wedge the tip of his tiny index finger into the lip of the top petal, his thumb into the bottom, and make the flower "snap." Remember?

Maura remembered as if it had been yesterday.

As always, the pain that came with that memory throbbed in her chest. Seeking diversion from the still-acute sorrow, she opened her eyes and gazed around the large yard, at the black plot for her vegetable garden from which Hank Peterson, her landlord, had already taken up the sod. The blocks of turf were already decomposing grass-side down in the compost heap Hank had constructed in the far corner of the lot. Along the fence separating her yard from her new neighbors grew hollyhocks and lilac bushes that would bloom later in May. And at the front of the lot, beneath a black walnut tree, stood her house. Hers in the sense she leased it and had an option to buy it someday. It was a small place, a cottage really, but big enough for her and her son. Big enough for their future together.

Finally a real home. Maura's fingers sank more deeply into the damp earth. *Yes, it's been a long time, Wayne.* Two years of apartment habitation on the outskirts of Soldier Creek—on the outskirts of life, it seemed—during which she'd existed in a state of perpetual worry. Over Davey, over money, over living. She realized, though, that two years was actually very little time in the scheme of things.

And yet it was an eternity in which to live alone, without the husband she thought she'd spend the rest of her life with.

She could still see him so clearly: lean and lanky, with a shock of straight blond hair, the front cowlicked in a way he'd passed on to his son. Even now she found it hard to believe Wayne was gone, killed in a freak accident at the co-op. Grain dust had spontaneously ignited—perhaps a wrench striking metal had produced a deadly spark in the volatile air, they said—and had blown up. The concussion had taken out windows in a blockwide radius, and killed Wayne Foster.

Startled out of her musings by the appearance of two Red Wing boots planting themselves next to her, Maura looked up. The morning sun blocked out the features of the person standing beside her. She shaded her eyes from the glare but still could make out only a tall figure, a man, weight relaxed on one leg, one hand propped against a hip, the other dangling at his side. The frame looked familiar, its dimensions once known to her.

Wayne?

Maura blinked back the moisture filming her eyes from squinting into the sun. She gave her head a shake, disoriented. She'd been focusing so intently she was seeing ghosts. Besides, this man was built nothing like Wayne. Even in silhouette, he was broader through the chest and shoulders, sinewy rather than lean, though slim through the waist, hips and thighs. More than that, a physical, quite unspectral energy radiated from the figure that towered over her.

A shiver of alarm swept over her, so brief it had passed before she recognized it, like the nip in the spring breeze.

Have a care, Maura dear.

The man moved out of the path of the sun. Nate Farrell stood in front of her, a questioning brow raised at her expression. "Maura?"

"Oh, Nate!" She gave a nervous laugh at her hallucinations. "I thought..." She shook her head again. "I was sitting here dreaming so hard I didn't know who you were for a moment."

"Dreaming?" Nate dropped to his haunches in front of her, elbows on his knees. He removed his green-and-white billed cap, its front advertising a seed-corn hybrid, and held it loosely between his clasped hands. Rays glinted off his burnished mahogany hair, shot through with traces of silver at his temples. Though closely cropped, it still curled attractively against his head.

"What does somebody up to her elbows in dirt dream about?" Nate asked in the imperturbable, thoughtful way Maura recalled as being so like him, though it had been a long time since she'd had a private conversation with him. He had a reputation for being remote, contained and therefore unapproachable. That was probably what had disturbed her a moment ago.

Maura smiled at his manner and at her ridiculous overreaction. *It's just Nate Farrell,* she told the whisper of warning in her head.

She mirrored his serious expression, which was nonetheless unsettling in its intensity. "Oh, I dream about the usual things. Tomatoes and squash, carrots and onions," she answered. "You know."

As intended, she made him smile, his eyes crinkling at the corners as his somber air dropped away. Lit with mirth, Nate's eyes became the most gorgeous blue-gray she'd ever seen, and twice as disconcerting as when solemn. They stood out in his handsome face with its high cheekbones, narrow nose and the Farrell chin, clefted in a fascinating manner that she hadn't had the inclination to note in the opposite sex in many a blue moon.

You've been too long without a man, Maura thought wryly. At his smile alone, she felt a flutter of pure attraction brush her cheeks and make them glow.

"I'd say your dreams are a tad bizarre, Maura," Nate responded.

"Well, I'll admit to going quietly but divinely mad right now." She lifted her fist and let a trickle of the clumpy soil sift to the ground. "It's going to feel so good to work the land again, *my* land."

He glanced around at the fifteen-by-twenty patch that had been prepared for tilling. "You sure this is enough land to satisfy your urges?" he asked.

"Urges?" For one moment, she wondered if he'd detected the direction of her unruly thoughts. Then she grasped his meaning. "Oh, my *gardening* urges. Yes, well, I'm a Master Gardener now," she said, her air of importance tempered with a smile. "I can't have an ordinary, run-of-the-mill garden patch, now can I?"

"I wouldn't know," Nate answered. "What in tarnation is a Master Gardener?"

"Well, don't tell Davey—he thinks it means I'm one step down from being a ninja or something—but I'm working with the university extension service to teach home horticulture in this area." She watched an earthworm wriggle from the soil under her hands.

"Really?" He looked surprised as he scrubbed the edge of his index finger against his notched chin. "I didn't realize you had such an interest in gardening."

"Oh, yes. I've always loved it." Maura nodded, the flat-brimmed coolie hat on her head bobbing. "And I'll love talking about it and teaching others." She jabbed her finger into the dirt and nudged the earthworm toward its new hidey-hole. "I hope to hold workshops for children at the new library, too. Workshops like—" she pointed to the shiny, red-brown worm "—'The Gardener's Friend.'"

Nate chuckled. "Did the city council realize they'd be getting a Master Gardener and librarian rolled into one when they hired you?"

"No. Think they'll mind?"

"I think they got a bargain."

"Thanks for the tip." Maura laughed. "I'll remember that when raise time comes around."

The smile faded from Nate's face. "It's good to see you doing so well, Maura," he said quietly.

"Thanks. I'm very excited about my job. And this house." She wrinkled her nose in faint embarrassment as she realized how she'd been rattling on to Nate, who was really not much more than a casual acquaintance. Yet he seemed truly interested.

"You should be, you're getting back on your feet and making a new start."

"Yes, I think I finally am," she said candidly. "It's been a long time since I've felt able to look ahead, you know...."

She let her voice trail off, reluctant to reexperience the circumstances that had caused her so much pain. Glancing up, she found Nate scrutinizing her, as if their conversation indeed held much more weight than just small talk. She looked away quickly. He was so intense it was disturbing.

But he's always been that way.

With that thought, Maura remembered a time when she'd seen this man at his most intense yet least contained. Out of control. The unconscious recollection of that episode had produced her apprehensive reaction earlier, she realized. It had been a long time since she'd thought of the incident, almost as if she'd purposely banished it from her mind.

For the truth was that Nate Farrell and his intensity *had* made an impression on her once—a definite and adverse impression.

Nate broke the silence between them. "So now your green thumb's prickling and twitching like a divining rod," he remarked so offhandedly she wondered if she'd imagined the look in his eyes.

Was he teasing her? She cast him a sidelong glance. His face revealed nothing, neither mirth nor earnestness. "You farm your own family's land, Nate. Surely you understand the feeling."

He shifted his weight to his other leg. "Well, I don't exactly wallow in the spring thaw, but I'll admit to feeling restless to get out in my fields each year. There's something satisfying in plowing that winter-crusted surface, turning it over and seeing how it pales against the rich color underneath." She watched in fascination as he changed again, his blue-gray eyes losing their laser sharpness and becoming suddenly tranquil, as she knew hers often did when her mind's eye pictured the fruits of her labor.

He does understand, she realized.

Then abruptly Nate snapped out of his daydream, shot her a self-conscious look and cleared his throat. "Of course, you probably heard, uh, about the way I've been plowing."

Maura opened her mouth, then shut it again as she saw a flush creep across his cheekbones. Yes, she had heard that

Nate, now fully in charge of the Farrell land, was implementing techniques and planting alternative crops that went against the grain of some of the more traditional ways of farming. In fact, he had been subjected to rather impassioned criticism for it. "Organic hippie stuff" or some such, she'd heard them describe his new methods. And they'd been calling him "Crazy Nate," those who indulged in that sort of thing. She had no doubt his reserved, off-putting personality had fed the fire.

Maura herself made it a point to ignore gossip, but a small town invariably provided the fertile ground for such goings-on. Folk were generally well-meaning, yet it remained that anything or anyone different was scrutinized, whether it was a body's business to do so or not.

A surge of respect for Nate rose in her, for having the courage to break out of the mold. The feeling was followed closely by a sense of kinship with him. Wayne had never experienced this deep commitment to the land, the respect for an invaluable resource. He'd never understood how her feelings went far beyond the economic concerns of producing vegetables for their table or a feminine desire to pretty up the yard. It was a need to give as good as she got, a personal thing understood at a gut level by those who shared it, incomprehensible to those who didn't.

It struck her that in the coming months she, too, would be introducing some relatively innovative ideas in gardening to the townspeople. And if he'd been labeled Crazy Nate, likely she'd end up being Mad Maura.

She opened her mouth once more to express such a sentiment, but Nate had already risen, knees cracking. Again he studied her with that exceptional intensity and looked as if he wished he'd never started this conversation with her. It dawned on her that she had no idea why he'd even stopped by in the first place.

Then another warning, one she recognized this time, sounded in her head: *That boy's looking for a wife.* It was her father's voice, and he was talking about Nate.

What had made her think of that? she wondered. Maura shot Nate a nervous glance as her cheeks grew warm with a confounding heat, as if he'd heard the message as loudly as she had.

But Nate's expression was ever distant as he fit his cap on his head with a tug on its bill, palm anchoring it at the back. He reached a hand down to help her up. "Seeing as how you're itching to poke seeds into this ground, we'd better get it tilled, don't you think?"

"We?" She took his hand and scrambled to her feet. "I thought Hank was going to till the garden for me."

"He was, but he looked a little, ah, perturbed when I saw him up at the lumberyard this morning, so I volunteered to help him out."

Maura watched Nate walk to the driveway and wheel back the rented industrial-strength Rototiller. He squatted and began filling the machine's tank from a gas can.

"Hank, perturbed?" She had never seen the easygoing Hank in any posture except perfectly relaxed. Things just didn't bother him. "He should have told me if he was too busy. I don't mind plowing the garden myself."

Nate lifted his eyebrows. "Ever till a patch of land that's never been turned?"

"No."

"It's a little taxing."

"Oh." She'd noticed that Nate almost always spoke in understatement and so took his observation to mean it was *very* taxing to till virgin soil. But if he were implementing different methods in plowing in his farming, the aspiring horticulturist in her wondered why he wouldn't suggest using those methods in her garden. Maura almost asked, but something told her Nate would be decidedly closed to that topic at the moment.

He replaced the gas cap and wiped his hands on a rag. "Helping you put in this garden wasn't what was bothering Hank. When I saw him, he had Jonas busy measuring out a bunch of two-by-fours, mixing up paint and counting out nails so fast I thought someone's house had burned down. Seems Hank's in a little bit of a hurry to finish off Cora's basement as a den for himself.'' Nate stood and hooked two fingers around the wood pull on the starter cord. ''I guess for an old bachelor like Hank, it's kind of hard to get used to living with someone after having unlimited privacy for so long. I imagine he feels like he needs a little space right now.''

''I imagine,'' Maura said drolly, ''being married to Cora Lawsen would be a strain on even the most sociable of men.'' Hardly a harridan, Cora Lawsen Peterson nonetheless was used to having her way.

Everyone had been surprised when the sixtyish Hank had proposed last fall, married Cora this spring and moved into her severely organized home a month ago. He'd left vacant the little house he had lived in alone for years, and he'd been glad to put it into Maura's capable hands. He'd even agreed to make certain improvements at little or no cost to her. The vegetable garden was the first of these projects.

Maura nodded her head. ''You just keep on helping Hank out, Nate. I don't want him deciding life with Cora isn't to be borne and coming back to take my house from me.''

That brought out his smile again, in devastating force. She *would* have to take care, she realized even while she grinned at Nate, glad to be back on relatively easy footing with him again.

Nate started up the Rototiller in a cloud of exhaust fumes and was soon making slow progress through the dense loam. Watching the machine buck and lunge even in Nate's capable hands, Maura understood how difficult it would have been for her to till the garden the first year, and how great a favor he was doing her by taking charge of the chore.

She helped him by picking rocks out of the turned soil, then spreading the expensive bagged peat she'd purchased. It would be a while before her compost heap would provide much economical organic matter for fertilizing the garden, and Maura was anxious to get her garden in. Even now in early May, it was nearly too late to put in cool-weather crops like lettuce and spinach.

A few hours later, Nate had tilled and re-tilled the ground, breaking up the larger clumps and working in the peat. Even with the crisp spring breeze, he'd removed his shirt and was perspiring freely. Maura pitched in wherever she saw the opportunity but often could do nothing more than make sure his way was clear and offer drinks of cold water when he paused to rest.

Yes, she reflected after some time watching him, Nate Farrell was one finely built man. She openly studied his muscled back as he drove the Rototiller in one direction and studied his chest less openly when he plowed a row toward her. The contained strength that was so much a part of his personality was physically evident in the way he handled the tiller, in his stance, which seemed as firmly set as a steel pylon. As she recalled, years ago he'd been quite a source of speculation among the teenage girls in Soldier Creek with his strong, silent, and therefore mysterious demeanor. She could see why even today he remained the subject of feminine conjecture, if Lou Ann's Beauty Parlor was any gauge.

Maura felt that same memory creep up on her, a memory that, she now realized, she'd held at arm's length for many years, though she couldn't say why she had done so. Likely because it would have served no purpose to dwell on a man who'd touched her young life so briefly. Not when she'd married another man.

With a start, Maura found Nate watching her as she stared at him. She turned away self-consciously, busying herself with spreading more peat.

Honestly, she had to corral her wandering thoughts and quit ogling him like prime show stock! Quite obviously, Maura reflected, she *was* coming out of her two-year-long stupor.

"Mama?"

Maura looked up. Davey, her son, stood at the partially open screen door on the back porch. He blinked owlishly, looking even more owlish in the black framed glasses he'd worn since the surgery to correct his crossed eye.

As always, Maura thought the glasses made him look unusually vulnerable. And, as always, it wrung her protective mother's heart. Those plastic lenses had become almost a shield of security for him, and he removed them only when sleeping.

"Hi, honey. Did you have a good rest?" She knew better than to intimate that he had napped, since big boys of five did not "nap." Normally Davey didn't, but with the excitement of the move over the past week, he had been cranky as a bear this morning. She'd suggested after breakfast that he might benefit from a little quiet time in his room. Five minutes later she'd found him passed out on his bed.

Clearly still groggy, Davey nodded in answer to her question and started down the steps and across the yard to investigate.

Nate paused in his work, running a bandanna over his shiny face. "Durn, Maura, if I'd known he was sleeping, I would've come back later instead of making all this racket."

She turned to him, her back to Davey. "Don't worry," she assured him in a low voice, "he was still dead to the world when I checked him half an hour ago."

Davey had reached her side, and he leaned his head against her thigh, yawning. She laid her palm over his forehead and brushed back his hair, a bright gold so like Wayne's. The cowlick sprang up like a cock's comb.

Maura noticed Nate's face lost all trace of its usual reserve as he smiled at the boy. "Just waking up, pardner?" he asked.

Davey nodded, squinting up at the tall man much as she must have earlier this morning.

"I don't think you know Nate, honey," Maura said. "Mr. Farrell farms south of Soldier Creek when he isn't helping us out with our garden patch."

Davey continued to stare at Nate thoughtfully. He scrunched his nose in a habit he'd acquired that pushed the bridge of his glasses infinitesimally upward. "I know," he said after a moment, "you're Crazy Nate."

"David Wayne Foster!" Maura exclaimed. She shot a mortified glance at Nate, whose face again became a mask of detachment.

Where had Davey learned such a name? It must have been from that Tommy Lee, who'd lived in the apartment across from theirs before they moved here. She'd disliked the seven-year-old from the first and suspected the only reason he'd even deigned to address five-year-old Davey was that no children his own age would tolerate his bullying and mean disposition. And Davey, too shy to seek out friends of his own, had naturally been drawn in by the older boy. She'd tried to limit Davey's time with Tommy, but obviously she'd not succeeded.

Thank God she wouldn't have to worry any longer about Tommy's influence on her son, but that didn't help her now.

Too embarrassed to meet Nate's eyes again, Maura gave Davey a reproachful frown. "You know it's wrong to call names." She tucked her chin in an *I'm waiting* pose. She shouldn't have to remind him how to rectify the situation.

To her relief, Davey possessed the good conscience to lower his eyes and redden in sincere shame. He pulled away from her, standing on his own.

"I'm sorry, Mr. Farrell," he said. "I didn't mean it." He hesitated, shuffling his feet, then added, "I know I don't like it when someone calls me . . . calls me Four Eyes."

Maura said nothing as tears stung at the back of her own eyes. She could guess also who'd called him that, though Davey had never mentioned it to her.

She glanced up to find Nate's understanding gaze fixed on the boy. He smiled. "Then why don't I call you Dave and you can call me Nate?"

Davey's face transformed itself at the suggestion. It seemed he was to be forgiven *and* treated like a man all at once. The ultimate, in his judgment. His brown eyes lit up, and his mouth formed a hesitant smile. He nodded. "Okay, Nate."

"Okay, Dave." In that way males have of deprecating emotion, Nate reached out and tugged on the forelock that spouted from Davey's forehead in a golden geyser. The seriousness her son wore like a habit departed as he grinned and wagged his head abashedly.

He's starved for male companionship, Maura thought, not for the first time in the past few months. She could almost see the bond forming between her son and this man as it did when kindred souls encountered each other. And these two were peas in a pod: serious, intense to a fault. Davey had always been somewhat so but had grown more and more solemn over the past few years. Maura had worried about it more times than she cared to count. She'd hoped it stemmed mainly from his father's death, but lately she had begun to understand this trait governed her son's personality and always would.

And because of that fledgling comprehension, Maura suddenly had a glimpse into Nate's nature.

Still waters run deep. In both of them.

She caught Nate's eye and smiled her gratitude for smoothing over the difficult moment. She couldn't imagine he was used to dealing with little boys and their fragile egos, yet he'd handled the situation marvelously and likely at cost to his own ego.

Crazy Nate. How difficult it must be for him to realize the label had reached even the ears of a five-year-old boy. Maura fervently hoped Nate wasn't bothered by the talk in town, though she could tell to some extent he was, even with that sturdy personal armor of his.

She glanced at her watch. "Look at the time!" Rubbing her hopelessly grimy hands down the front of her equally hopeless jeans, she gestured with her head toward the house. "Go on in and change your shirt, honey, while I finish up with Nate. Your appointment at Lou Ann's is in half an hour."

The smile disappeared from Davey's face. His lower lip grew, making him the perfect image of his father when he was being stubborn. Wayne Foster would never be lost to her as long as she had his son.

"I don't want a haircut," he said stoutly.

"Now, Davey." Maura cast Nate a chagrined look. He probably thought her the worst mother in Soldier Creek to be raising such an obstinate, ill-mannered child. "We talked about this. I don't do a very good job of cutting your hair anymore, now that it's gotten so... thick, and you need to have someone who knows what they're doing give you a good cut. Lou Ann cuts my hair," she added, though the example was a lame one. Her long hair rarely needed more than a trim of the ends, nothing like what a little boy with a silver-dollar-sized cowlick required.

"But I don't *need* a haircut," Davey negotiated.

"Yes, you do. I thought we'd have a Maid Rite sandwich at the café afterwards," Maura said on another tack. Bribery, no less! But why was Davey being so stubborn?

A thought struck her. "I know Lou Ann and all the other ladies fuss over you, honey. You won't have to sit and wait for me. We'll get you in and out in no time, I promise."

She saw this assurance had not the least bit effect on the boy. She was trying to come up with another argument when Nate spoke up.

"You know," he said, giving Davey a measuring scrutiny before turning to Maura, "Ernie up at the barbershop usually does a pretty good job for me. Think he could handle a bristle brush like Dave's?"

Maura gave him a measuring look of her own as she tried to suppress a smile. Now, why hadn't she thought of that? Probably, she reasoned, because she felt as much reluctance at entering that bastion of masculinity as Davey did for invading Lou Ann's Beauty Parlor. Wayne had always gotten his hair cut at Ernie's, and she'd bet every man in town did. It just hadn't entered her mind to think Davey would find flowered cutting capes and pink chairs an intolerable affront to his developing male sensibilities.

She turned to find her son gazing up at her with undisguised longing. "I suppose I could take you to Ernie's," she said slowly, picturing the scenario quite clearly, having passed by it innumerable times: the usual collection of grizzled farmers in Osh-kosh work pants, sweat-rimmed, seedcorn caps on their heads, hashing and rehashing the weather from their posts near the plate-glass window; Ernie sitting high up on his barber chair, legs crossed and a goodly amount of pale, hairy shin showing between stocking and pant leg as he read the Des Moines *Register* for what was surely the third time that day. In her mind's eye she saw behind him, reflected in the mirror, ancient bottles of Lucky Tiger hair tonic and jars of Wildroot lining the shelf under faded advertisements for Clove, Teaberry and Black Jack gum.

The setting reeked of inviolable, age-old maleness. No wonder the option hadn't immediately popped to mind.

Again Nate must have sensed her dilemma. More for Davey's benefit than hers, she presumed, he smoothed his palm conspicuously over his nape. "You know, I was thinking I needed a little trim myself. How about I take Dave with me to Ernie's?"

This, Maura noticed, sent her son into silent fits of anticipation that she tried to ignore while judging the fairness of the situation.

"I couldn't ask you to do so much, Nate," she protested. "You've already spent quite a bit of time helping me."

"It won't take long, and I don't mind, Maura. I'm just about done here. And wouldn't you rather keep working on your garden?"

Maura's eyes rested wistfully on the wheelbarrow of old bricks Hank had obtained for her to edge her garden. Feeling herself wavering, she glanced back at Nate. "It seems such a personal thing, though, taking a little boy for his first barber-cut. And then taking him to the café, too. I don't want to impose on you."

He shrugged, and Maura watched the movement ripple the muscles in his strong shoulders and upper chest. She'd noted earlier the nice sprinkling of hair across that expanse of skin, and now she swallowed with difficulty before jerking her gaze upward. She met Nate's discerning eyes, the color of the irises blooming on the sunny side of the house.

Maura reddened. It really *had* been too long if seeing a man's chest produced such a reaction in her. What must he think of her, staring all the time?

He fixed her with one of those spellbinding, intense looks. "It's no imposition."

"Don't worry, Mama. I'll be good," Davey offered hopefully.

She broke eye contact with Nate only to find her son giving her an equally intense look. Over a haircut, for pity's sake.

Such a serious child. She would rather he spend time in the company of someone less like himself, who might encourage him by example to lighten up. But she could see her son wanted a man to take him to Ernie's. And though this man was practically a stranger, Nate was still preferable to a mother in this instance. The thought produced a sudden ache in her, a feeling of frustrated inadequacy, for she knew there would be many more such instances in their lives as she raised her son without a father. She hated to think she wasn't equipped to handle those situations alone.

And yet she *had* been searching for ways to promote Davey's independence, nearly as much as she'd sought ways to achieve her own.

She ruffled his blond hair tenderly. "I know you'll be good, honey. All right. Let me get my purse, and I'll give you some money."

"You don't need—" Nate began, but Maura cut him off.

"No, I insist. It won't take me a minute."

She rinsed her hands under the outdoor faucet and hurried to locate her billfold while Nate finished up with the tiller and wheeled it back to the garage for Hank to pick up and return to the rental place in nearby Newton. He was soaking his bandanna under the spout and freshening up when Maura returned a few minutes later.

As she bent to tuck a ten-dollar bill into the breast pocket of Davey's shirt, Maura eyed its somewhat grimy state. For Lou Ann's, she'd have made him change it. But she suspected at Ernie's he'd likely be in the main. And as for the crowd at the café . . . well, her son usually managed to wear some part of his lunch on his shirt anyway.

She straightened as Nate ambled over. "There's enough money for a haircut for Davey and a Maid Rite at Myra's for both of you." Embarrassment for both her and her son's behavior that morning still lay uppermost in her mind, what with Nate being so considerate, and she put a hand on his arm. "Nate—" She hesitated, not wanting Davey to overhear her.

Once again Nate sensed her quandary. He gave Davey a gentle push toward his pickup truck parked on the street. "Go on, pard. I'll catch up in a minute." He watched the boy trot off, then turned back to Maura. "Yes?"

She could think of no way to apologize for her own indiscretions but needed at least to make amends for Davey's. "I wanted to tell you that Davey never heard that . . . name from me. You know that, don't you?"

He stooped and picked up his shirt from the grass. "I know, Maura."

"And he will be good with you. He's really a very cooperative fellow. It's just that it's been a little tough for him lately, for us both."

"I *know,* Maura." His blue-gray eyes told her that he did. She wondered if many people ever saw what she did right now, that underneath Nate Farrell's reserve existed a wonderful warmth. But then she knew that, had felt that warmth once, though briefly. And she could see it now, when he dealt with Davey, and it touched her. One learned a lot about a man from the way he treated children, the elderly or animals. More than could be learned through years of acquaintance—or from an isolated incident long ago.

She gave him a shy smile. "He likes you."

"I like him," Nate answered simply, then shook his head. "I can't believe you were going to take that kid to the beauty parlor!"

The sight of his smiling face, so close to hers, brought another glow to her cheeks, which she covered with gruff orders. "Well, don't let him forget his manners. And *don't* let Ernie put anything slick on his hair." Anxiously she glanced after the boy, who'd bent down to pick up something in the yard. Davey stood and examined it, chin on his chest and stomach thrust out, making him look as if he still had a baby's paunch. Again a swell of maternal protectiveness rose in her.

She turned back to Nate. "Maybe I should go with you."

He made a small sound of exasperation. "Maura."

"I mean, it is his first real haircut."

"I'll have Ernie tie up a lock of Davey's hair in a pretty blue ribbon if you like."

She caught the twinkle in his eye and laughed. "That's not what I meant. It's just an awfully personal favor, Nate. And you've really done enough for me already."

Nate said nothing, but he slid on his shirt, buttoned it and stuffed its tails into his jeans, all the while holding her gaze with his. "I guess if I want to do a personal favor for you, Maura Foster," he finally said in his quiet manner, "I'll do it."

Did he have to look at her that way? As if he wanted to find her soul through her eyes? Maura had a sudden presentiment—or was it that memory again? Something told her that, if he chose to, Nate Farrell could get anything he really wanted with that unswerving focus. In his own time, in his own way.

Nate turned to follow Davey. When he reached him, he stooped and considered, with as much earnestness as the boy had himself, the object Davey held up. Even from several yards away, Maura saw the whole aspect of Nate's face change, soften, as he said something to Davey, who nodded, pocketing the bit of flotsam.

Yes, there was something undeniably touching seeing a man in this context. Touching... moving... and, she realized, completely thrilling. A rush of awareness hit her all at once.

Nate picked that exact moment to straighten and glance back at her. She felt he read in her eyes every wayward thought she'd experienced that morning.

And that he remembered, too.

Chapter Two

Nate entered Ernie's barbershop with the unfamiliar but not unappealing cargo of a little boy in tow. And he knew the minute he glanced around that he'd stepped into a brier patch of unpleasantness.

It was nearly noon and, in addition to the regulars who passed their days at Ernie's, the lunch-hour faction had gathered. This was made up of several old-timers who daily wended their way into town from various outlying farms in anticipation of the diversion of a hot lunch at Myra's and a few minutes of regurgitated gossip at Ernie's.

Like cows chewing cud, Nate reflected. He was of the private opinion that anyone who deemed gossip a female pastime had never been to Ernie's over the noon hour.

All talk ceased as soon as he and Davey stepped through the door. Nate acknowledged the group of five men in the corner with a nod of his head, offering neither encouragement nor discouragement of further exchanges.

"Hey there, Nate." Ernie folded his newspaper and climbed down from his red leather barber chair. He was a small, thin man who, despite hearing daily the indiscriminate speculations of his regulars, maintained a carefully neutral position by reading and rereading the paper from his perch high above the others.

Ernie bent at the waist, the heels of his hands on his knees, and regarded Davey solemnly. "And who's this big feller?"

Davey, obviously overcome by the foreign and rather daunting surroundings, stared back wordlessly.

"This here's Dave," Nate said, laying a reassuring palm on Davey's shoulder. "He's Maura Foster's—"

"That Wayne Foster's boy?" a loud voice interrupted.

Nate turned. Arvid Newley, fat and florid, overflowed on a straight-backed wooden chair in the corner. He overshadowed the men in the surrounding chairs in both physical stature and downright audacity.

Nate nodded. "Yes, Wayne's son," he said tersely, wondering why he was feeling so thin-skinned that Arvid's correction rankled. It was probably because Arvid had never extended to Nate the "civility" the rest of Soldier Creek had by criticizing him behind his back instead of to his face.

Arvid gestured with a meaty hand. "Come on over here, son, and let me get a look at you."

Though undoubtedly reluctant, Davey nonetheless shuffled over to within a few feet of Arvid.

The older man planted his palms on his thighs, his elbows cocked outward, and leaned forward, closing the distance between his face and Davey's.

"Lord, don't you look like your dad, with that lick of wild hair in the front." Arvid reached out with stubby fingers and pulled on Davey's forelock much the same as Nate had done earlier, although, Nate noticed, without the same effect. Instead of a grin, Davey cast his eyes down at the floor, his mouth set in a line. Clearly the boy was minding his manners at a cost. Nate felt a tug of empathy.

"Got your ma's look around the eyes," Arvid went on, oblivious to Davey's aggravation. "Can't hardly tell, though, with them glasses—"

Now it was Nate's turn to interrupt. "Let's get you up here, pard," he said smoothly, inserting his hands under the boy's armpits and boosting him into the high chair Ernie had vacated.

Arvid and his blamed mouth! Nate almost wished he'd let Maura take the kid to Lou Ann's. Better to be fussed over by a bunch of women than to have his looks picked apart by a tactless old coot like Arvid.

"So, what are we doing here today?" Ernie ceremoniously waved the red plastic cape like a bullfighter before settling it around Davey's small neck.

"Mama says I need a haircut," Davey said importantly, shoulders twitching against the curious sensation of the cape across them. "A *real* one."

The conversation resumed on the other side of the room, though Nate saw out of the corner of his eye that the intimate little vignette on this side was just too tempting for the older men to ignore.

Clearing his throat, Nate caught Ernie's attention. He scratched his nose with one finger and surreptitiously pointed skyward at his own hairline. "Uh, just a trim, Ernie."

The barber nodded. "I think we can manage a trim." He reached for Davey's glasses.

"No!" Two small hands, covered in red plastic, darted upward and clamped over the black frames. Evidently not anticipating this step in the haircutting process, Davey shot an imploring look at Nate. Surprised by the emphatic protest, Ernie also glanced to Nate for help.

Poor little mite, Nate thought, grasping the situation at once. Aware of the corner contingent, he took a step forward, smiling confidently.

"Say, Dave, why don't I hold on to those for you?" he suggested as he tugged the glasses from the little boy's grasp.

Obviously with misgiving, Davey let him, his eyes following Nate's movements as he folded the earpieces together and tucked the frames into his breast pocket. Crossing one ankle over the other, Nate settled back against the counter, effectively blocking the boy's view of himself in the mirror and hopefully from the probing perusal coming from the men in the corner. Davey blinked myopically but made no further protest as he looked up at Nate, brows puckered above solemn eyes.

Just like his mother's, Nate thought as Ernie began snipping away. *Big, brown and soulful.*

He should never have volunteered to help her this morning, for within minutes he'd found himself again falling under the spell of those eyes. *No, not a spell,* Nate mentally amended. That implied Maura Foster tried to reel him in, knew she could. But it was because her effect was so unintentional that he'd felt the hook in his lip. And knowing that effect, over the years he'd stayed away.

It had happened before, just this way, most recently last spring. Last year the tornado that destroyed his parents' home had distracted him from her. He wondered what would do the trick this time, because the fact of the matter was that Maura Foster was just too durn appealing. He'd always thought so. She had an old-fashioned way about her, sweet and wholesome. She even looked wholesome, with that long, honey blond hair braided in a halo around her head. She had the kind of skin that was unfashionably pale but perfect, and a pink mouth he couldn't imagine any color of lipstick could enhance.

Nate jumped when Arvid spoke, hitting close to the direction of his thoughts, "Didn't know you and Maura Foster were particular friends there, Nate."

Nate stifled a sigh, thinking he'd be durn glad when his rotation at the rumor mill was up. But if people didn't have his farming to talk about, they'd start speculating about his private life. Neither option appealed to him, but if he had his druthers, he'd put up with people running down his reputation rather than matchmaking.

He shot a look at Davey to see if he'd heard Arvid's comment. Hard to tell. The boy seemed to be concentrating on holding himself stock-still, eyes swiveling left, then right, then upward in tandem with Ernie's progress.

"Just doing a favor for a neighbor," Nate said easily.

"In fact," Arvid went on, "you and Wayne Foster had a bit of a dis-pute over Maura at one time, didn'cha?"

Nate felt himself grow hot around the collar, though he managed to keep his face blank. Blast Arvid for having a memory like an elephant! "That was years ago," he said, hoping to put an end to the subject.

"Took Wayne out of baseball practice for a whole week," Arvid informed his cronies. "Lord, that boy had an arm on him! Do you remember that one game against Inaville . . ."

Their conversation drifted on to other subjects, and Nate expelled a breath of relief before his mouth settled into a pensive frown. Yes, he thought, there'd once been a quite personal confrontation between him and Wayne Foster. And that one time had taught him, more than any other since, that it was better to walk away, as he knew he would from Arvid and his gang. As he should have from Maura this morning.

But today, for the first time in two years, he thought she might be taking an interest in life and perhaps in him. He'd felt it, *known* it, when he caught her staring at him. It was obvious he appealed to her, as well, though he had long ago realized that something else about him, even stronger, did not appeal to her and never had.

And that's why he'd stayed away.

Ernie was nearly finished, had done a pretty good job, too, except for that cowlick spraying over Davey's forehead like a rooster's tail. The barber and Nate eyed the rebellious shock of hair. *Just like his father's,* Nate thought wryly.

"Say there, Nate." Arvid broke into his thoughts again.

Nate met the older man's eyes over the top of Davey's head. "Arvid?"

"I was just wondering how your planting's going. You planning on beans in that field down by the creek?"

Nate watched as Ernie unsnapped the cape from Davey's neck and scooped it aside. Blond hair sprinkled like glitter across the dark linoleum floor.

"Nope," Nate said succinctly, and immediately became annoyed with himself for answering at all. Again he hoped the boy wouldn't notice the direction the conversation had taken, but Davey looked at him suddenly, anxiously, and Nate knew he'd detected the strained tone of his monosyllabic reply.

"No?" Looking puzzled, Arvid glanced at his companions. "Getting kind of late for corn, ain't it? Unless you're gonna plant that amaranth or that tofu stuff there, like you did next to your place." A thought seemed to smite Arvid with the force of a lightning bolt. "You can't be thinking of letting that good patch of land go to pot like you did that other one near your folks', can you?"

With effort, Nate stifled the explanation that would do no good. *You'd think I was trying to turn water to wine.*

What was it to them if he wanted to plant alternative crops like amaranth grain or tofu soybeans instead of the regular kind? And was it anyone's business but his own if he was untiling the bits and pieces of his land that had always been marginally productive anyway? It wasn't as if some of these ideas hadn't been around for a while, but it was a testimony to Iowa stubbornness that the majority of farmers still resisted even familiarizing themselves with them. *They'd* never grow a crop they'd have to go to the trouble of finding a whole different market for! And letting useful farmland turn to marsh? That wasn't crazy—it was plain stupid!

"Uh, none of that stuff," Nate said, grateful for the distraction of Ernie's going for a jar of some kind of hair goo. No, Nate knew better than to try to explain to Arvid the organic-and sustainable-farming concepts he was implementing. Arvid would think he'd *really* lost it if he started talking about recharging the aquifer by returning some of his land to wetlands. Much better to have the town wonder if Nate Farrell was crazy than to confirm it for certain.

"Now, Arvid," Jasper Quinn said, "maybe Nate here just forgot to plant that land. Just like it must've slipped his mind to do his fall plowing last year."

"Do tell!" Arvid exclaimed. "Your pa know you're day-dreaming 'stead of farming, Nate?" This commentary produced a chuckle from the group.

Don't dignify the remark with a response. He could almost predict what would happen. By tomorrow he'd be known as Lazy Nate instead of Crazy Nate. He again said nothing as he fastened his eyes on Davey, who had reached up and found, somewhat to his amazement, that he'd retained both ears.

Dipping inside his pocket, Nate produced the black glasses and slid them on the boy's face. Only then did he step aside, giving Davey a view of his newly shorn hair.

Solemnly Davey regarded himself in the mirror. One side of his mouth curled dubiously upward, denting his freckled cheek. He glanced to Nate for confirmation.

Nate nodded. "Pretty sharp, pardner."

Davey jumped about three inches off his seat at the whisk of soft bristles across his neck as Ernie swept the remaining hair from Davey's shoulders with a small, round brush. His face completely straight, Ernie swooped the brush into the back of Davey's collar with a swish that surely tickled. The boy flashed a heart-touching grin, and Nate found himself grinning back.

Such an impressionable kid. Suddenly he wanted more than anything to get Davey out of there before more of Arvid's thoughtless observations hit those sensitive ears.

Hoping it didn't look as though he hurried, Nate set the boy on his feet. He reached for the bill in Davey's pocket and waited with barely contained patience for Ernie to make change. Pocketing it himself, Nate was shepherding the boy toward the door and deliverance when Davey piped up in a voice that pealed like a cowbell, "What about you, Nate? Aren'cha getting a haircut, too?"

Nate stopped, his back to the group, the tips of his fingers resting lightly on Davey's shoulders. The boy looked up at him with those wide, guileless eyes.

Just like his mother's.

Nate felt a flush creep up his neck. Hang it all! He couldn't help thinking if he hadn't literally jumped at the chance to help Maura out this morning, he wouldn't be standing here now in this durn awkward situation with her son staring up at him and him feeling like he couldn't bear it if the kid got an earful of Arvid's slander.

Nate struggled with the dilemma of looking as if he was either running or had lied to the boy about needing a haircut himself. It struck him that he didn't care what Arvid and the rest of them thought, but he cared, probably more than he should, what this five-year-old thought.

He opened his mouth to speak, but Davey had already filled the breach. "I'm kinda hungry, though. Can we go eat first?"

The brown eyes remained as innocent as before, though Nate caught a hint of comprehension in their depths.

"Sure, Dave. Let's walk over to Myra's." He turned and touched the edge of a finger to the bill of his cap. "Ernie. Boys." And he took his leave.

Out on the sidewalk, Nate spent a moment willing his frustration to dissipate. He should never have put himself in a position of defending himself—or caring to. But even though the remarks had dwindled through the winter, as if in dormancy, today had shown him that, with the return of spring and the visible evidence of "Farrell's Folly," he'd again become the center of criticism. Truth was, he'd never paid much mind to what people said, cared little whether they were even accurate in their assumptions about him. But lately he found himself caring for the effect on his family, and now, he realized, for this boy and his mother. Maura had obviously heard the talk. He wondered what she thought—that he was crazy? Or maybe she thought he was just Iowa stubborn in a whole other way. Not sticking to one's guns stubborn. More like needlessly sticking one's neck out stubborn.

Nate felt the familiar response, ingrained in him over the years, to convince himself that he cared not a whit what people thought, what *she* thought.

But the fact of the matter was he didn't want Maura or her son thinking of him as Crazy Nate.

Deep in contemplation, Nate paused automatically at the curb before crossing the road. He was surprised by the sensation of a small, warm hand fitting itself into his. Nate glanced down. Davey carefully looked both ways, though it was highly unlikely that the sole vehicle moseying up Main Street would fail to brake for an inattentive pedestrian. But the boy had obviously been taught to stop, look and listen.

Nate wondered if taking his hand was part of the routine or if Davey had added that touch of reassurance on his own.

He gave the small hand a squeeze as its warmth stole through him, the tightness in his chest easing. He could get used to this, he realized. But if he were smart, he would fulfill the rest of his obligation today and in the future leave a wide berth around Maura Foster and her son.

If he were smart.

A rush of hot air hit Maura's face as she opened the oven door and reached with pot-holder-covered hands for the two casseroles on the lower rack. Setting each dish on an unlit burner, she slid the door shut and inhaled the delicious aroma. Gravy bubbled around nicely browned biscuits atop cubed beef, carrots, onions and potatoes. It was only Boy Scout stew, but she hoped a bachelor like Nate would find the prospect of a hot, homemade meal a welcome difference from his usual fare.

Maura had finally decided this afternoon, after waffling for a day, that she should thank Nate with more than words for his help with the garden and with Davey. Had he been any other neighbor, she'd have cooked up something the same afternoon, but it occurred to her that she felt slightly different about Nate Farrell.

She was still puzzled by her response to him and why it had come upon her now of all times. After all, it wasn't as if she hadn't known him for years. Although, she realized, she really didn't *know* Nate Farrell. She wondered if anyone did, outside of his family or his best friend and brother-in-law, Drew Barnett. The other day she'd had glimpses of the man behind the stoic facade, but he put up a formidable guard. And no wonder. She cringed whenever she remembered Davey's remark and her own indiscreet ogling.

Maura flicked off the oven. It was, as she'd told herself before, probably nothing more than her hormones waking up after so long. She was glad, on the one hand, to think she might be returning to the land of the living. Smelling the flowers, as it were. Her new interest in everything, including Nate Farrell, demonstrated to her she was finally healing. And more than anything, Maura wanted to believe she was returning to normal.

Yet still she vacillated over extending to him a token of her appreciation. She had no confidence he'd welcome it. Except... though nothing explicit had been said, she'd caught the returned interest in his gaze, since there was no doubt in her mind that he'd noticed the way she stared at him in a most encouraging way. She realized suddenly that baking for Nate implied certain ambitions, like wanting to make her way into this man's heart through his stomach! And that was *not* her aim. Not at all. She was too busy seeing to Davey and their survival to even think of such nonsense.

Maura eyed the stew with dismay. Well, it wasn't as if she had much choice in the way of thanks to offer Nate. Her better skills ran to the domestic. "Of course," she muttered, "I could always extend him an extra week's grace on his library rentals."

Maura grinned in spite of herself. She was making too much of the whole situation. The stew would be fine.

She turned as Doreen Foster knocked briefly at the back door before entering the house, Davey ushered along in front of her.

"Here we are," Wayne's mother said amiably, patting her hair as if the breeze would have had any success in disturbing the stiff hairdo, the silvery gold color of corn silk. She set a small paper sack on the kitchen table. "And here's the notions you needed. Two spools of thread and some binding tape, both green. Don't you look pretty!" she exclaimed as Maura slid off her apron. "Is that new?"

She smoothed down the skirt of the simple dress in a gay cotton print. "Yes. It's one I made to wear at the library."

"You're not going to work now, are you, Mama?" Davey asked a little apprehensively.

"No, honey," she answered. Though she'd explained how their schedule would change over the summer, she knew Davey was still confused on the details. As it stood, beginning Monday she would work at the library from ten to six on weekdays, plus Thursday evenings and Saturday afternoons. Davey would spend part of the time with her at the library and part with his grandmother until he started kindergarten that fall.

"I just had a bath after all my hard work today and felt like dressing up a bit," she explained to her son. She refrained from mentioning that the possibility of seeing Nate had influenced that decision.

"Did you get everything done you wanted to?" Doreen asked.

"Just about." Doreen had taken time off today from her job doing the books for the co-op, now rebuilt after the accident, to take Davey to town so Maura would have one last afternoon free of interruptions. "The garden's in, that's the main thing I wanted to get out of the way before I started at the library. I can run those curtains up in the evenings after work."

Maura had discovered that handyman Hank had left the house structurally perfect but without a hint of decoration. She'd spent the week since moving in painting and papering as much as her budget would allow, and she was quite satisfied with her efforts.

Her son, it seemed, was not. "Stinks, Mama," he said, pinching his nose.

"I know, honey. It's paint. It'll go away."

"Oh, let me look," Doreen said as she popped into the next room.

"Tell me what you think," Maura called. She had nearly finished her bedroom today by painting it an off-white she would accent with pale green curtains.

Her mother-in-law returned to the kitchen. "I like it," she said. "It really opens up that room."

"I hope so." Maura laughed. "I don't know how any of these rooms could appear any smaller."

The one problem with the house was that it was extraordinarily tiny. Still, Maura had no complaints. It *was* small, but she needed nothing bigger. It was home. And it was hers.

"Well, this place is big enough for the two of you," Doreen said, echoing her thoughts. "And now you're only a few blocks away, without the highway between, like the apartment was. When Mama starts work next week, you'll be able to walk over to Grandma's all by yourself, won't you, Davey boy?"

"You betcha," the youngster agreed, using one of Doreen's catch phrases.

Maura smiled at the two of them. Never was her son more at ease than with his grandmother. She wondered if Davey remembered how his father had called him by that nickname. *Davey boy.*

And she'd always been *Maura dear.*

Little details like these always brought Wayne back so vividly to her, as Doreen herself did. Not only was she built like Wayne, tall and thin, but Doreen's lighthearted personality matched her deceased son's in so many ways.

The older woman had been her lifesaver over the past two years. Due to her father's job, Maura's own family had moved to Spokane after she and Wayne married. Wayne, his parents and his brother Kenny had provided the love and closeness she missed.

Then Wayne's father had passed away, leaving Doreen a widow at fifty. Kenny got a job selling farm implements, which kept him on the road most of the time. And Wayne had been killed, leaving Maura a widow at twenty-eight.

So the two women cleaved to each other, having lost both husband and son. Maura knew she'd never be able to repay Doreen for the emotional support the older woman had given her and Davey.

She glanced at her son. He had settled himself in a chair at the table and was putt-putting a Hot Wheels car along its edge.

She looked closer. "Is that a new one of those things?" She lowered her brows at her mother-in-law. "Doreen, you'll spoil him rotten yet," she admonished with an indulgent smile. She couldn't find it in her heart to seriously reprove the older woman for pampering Davey. Besides being a grandmother's prerogative, Maura knew it helped to lessen Doreen's own heartache to care for her son's son.

"Phooey," she said in response to Maura's comment as she picked up a fork and sampled from one of the dishes. "Mmm. You'll be eating well tonight, Davey boy." She paused, puzzled. "Two stews?"

"Yes. I was planning to take one to... a neighbor who helped out tilling the garden for me." She had no idea why she found herself reluctant to mention Nate to Doreen, but she hoped her vague explanation would satisfy her mother-in-law.

Unfortunately it didn't. "You mean Hank?" Doreen's relatively unlined forehead puckered. "He's got Cora cooking for him now."

Maura turned away, pulling from the cupboard the wicker basket that fit the bottom of the casserole dish. "Not Hank." Again she hesitated and wondered why she did so.

"Nate helped us, Gran'ma," Davey spoke up helpfully. "Yesterday when he took me for my haircut. 'Member I told you?"

"Oh," Doreen said. From the corner of her eye, Maura saw the other woman's thoughtful countenance as she took in the fresh dress, the jaunty blue ribbon tied to the end of the thick blond braid lying on Maura's shoulder, the lovingly prepared stew. The older woman's forehead became a collection of concerned creases.

Maura wondered if Doreen had heard the talk around town about Crazy Nate. She hoped not as a strange indignation and protectiveness crept up on her. Nate had a right to farm as he saw fit.

"Excuse me, Maura," Doreen said in a suddenly formal voice, setting the fork down. "I shouldn't have just waltzed in here and stuck my nose into the nice dish you're taking to a neighbor."

"That's okay. Either casserole will do. And it's not much, just a stew. But Hank asked Nate to give us a hand, and he was kind enough to take Davey to Ernie's for me," she explained a little defensively. Sticking up for herself or for Nate? "I thought this would be a nice way to thank him."

She hoped Doreen would attribute the rosiness in her cheeks to the heat in the kitchen, though she herself knew it was more. It occurred to her she was reluctant to mention Nate's innocent offer of help because of her not-so-innocent reaction to him. Since Wayne's death—indeed, since she had first known Doreen—never had Maura demonstrated an interest in men, except for Wayne. To show an awareness now, even on a casual level, seemed almost a disloyalty, as if she'd forgotten Wayne.

I haven't forgotten, Maura thought. No, she hadn't, but deep in her heart she knew that more than anything she needed to put the past behind her and get on with her life.

She concentrated on slipping the dish into its woven holder. Taking a deep breath, she said as matter-of-factly as possible, "I was just waiting for you two to get back so I could run this out to Nate's. I thought if I got it out there before five, even if he were still out in the fields, I could leave it where he'd see it so he didn't start cooking something else."

"Tell him about my nickel," Davey put in.

"If he's even there, honey, I will." Maura glanced at the clock above the stove. It was nearly five now. "I'll stay only a few minutes, though, Doreen, if you'll watch Davey for a little while longer." She smiled at her mother-in-law, hoping the older woman would read in her eyes just how benign this whole matter was. "Why don't you wait and have supper with us?"

"Yeah, Gran'ma, stay," Davey said. "Then you can play Chutes and Ladders with me afterwards."

Doreen smiled, her face losing the bemused expression of a few minutes ago as she regarded her grandson. "Is that all I'm good for, young man, games and toys?"

Davey grinned and shrugged his small shoulders, looking the image of his father at his most roguish.

Maura picked up the still-hot casserole dish and held it gingerly as she swung around and raised her eyebrows at her mother-in-law. "I told you you'd spoil him."

They laughed, and Maura felt her apprehensions slip away. *See? Things are the same as they always were,* she wanted to reassure both her son and her mother-in-law. But the words wouldn't come to her lips.

Depressing the latch with her elbow, Maura shoved the door open with her hip. "Back soon." She'd promise that much.

Though only a few minutes past five, Nate's pickup was parked in the driveway, indicating that he was indeed home. Slightly unnerved, Maura pulled up behind the truck. She realized she'd been trusting fate to play the deciding card in

determining whether her motivations in coming here tonight were purely charitable. And fate had just made a decisive move.

Honestly, she thought with exasperation. Living the past
two years of her life in mental isolation had made her as introspective as a nun. She was making too much of an absolutely harmless situation. *Knock on the door, give him the
casserole, chat a few minutes and leave.* What was so piv-
otal about that?

But she did indeed want something, if only to see Nate for
a moment, to see just once the sun break through from behind the clouds, which was how she thought of his smile.
Maura climbed the steps to the back porch of the small, tidy
farmhouse and rapped forcefully on the aluminum door.
There was no answer.

She frowned and turned, scanning the outbuildings for a
sign of Nate. Perhaps he tended stock this time of day. She
wouldn't want to interrupt him. So she *was* destined to miss
him.

Setting the glass dish on the wide wooden railing, Maura
rubbed the pads of her fingers against her palm as she wondered whether she should open the door and take the casserole inside. If she left it on the step, the barn cats might get
into it.

Maura searched the yard again for signs of Nate. She'd
better take the dish inside. Entering his home uninvited,
however, was not a familiarity she felt comfortable with. It
was just too intentional, too... personal.

But if I want to do a personal favor for you, I'll do it.

"Hello, Maura."

She swung around, nearly upsetting the stew. Through the
screen in the door she saw a dark shadow standing within
the dim interior of the house. The setup seemed a repeat of
their meeting the other day and magnified her misgivings
about being there.

"Oh, Nate." She laid a steadying hand on the dish and one over her heart as it drummed her surprise. "I thought you must be out in the barn or something."

"I was in the shower." He opened the door, and she saw that, quite literally, he'd just stepped from there. He was shirtless and barefoot, wearing only a pair of jeans. Drops of water clung to the dark hair on his chest, which he blotted absently with a towel. Bracing the door open with his foot, he finger combed his hair with the other hand as he looked down at her with heart-stopping intensity.

The air went dead in her lungs.

Nervously she indicated the stew. "I've brought something to thank you for your help the other day."

At his inquiring expression, she lifted the lid, releasing a billow of aromatic steam. Nate bowed and inhaled appreciatively, and Maura found her eyes focusing on a bead of water trailing its way from temple to jaw to neck to its final destination in the nest of dark hair at the base of his throat.

She swallowed. Well, she hadn't foreseen this scenario, by any means.

"It's just a Boy Scout stew," she said, minimizing her effort as she had with Doreen, though she couldn't help but feel a rush of feminine achievement at the look of pleasure on Nate's face. She'd been right to extend this thanks to him.

"Mmm," he murmured. He opened the door wider for her entry. "Don't just stand there, woman, bring that in here."

She lifted the casserole and ducked beneath his arm into the house. Under cover of fussing with the hot dish, she regained her composure by examining her surroundings.

Nate's home looked much the same as Hank's had before she moved in to it. Everything was in its place, but the entire kitchen wore an air of austerity. She recalled that, as with many farming families, the Farrells had acquired this house when they'd purchased the surrounding land years ago. It was a much less charming dwelling than the main

house a few miles away, occupied by his parents. Yet it had
its possibilities, Maura thought, just as Hank's house had.
All it needed was a touch of color to break the monotony.

Deep within a spontaneous reverie in which she stenciled
a cheerful border around the room, Maura jumped at Nate's
touch on her arm. "Oh!"

"Caught you again, didn't I?" he said.

"Again?"

"Daydreaming. You were a million miles away."

Apparently she had been lost to the world for at least a
few minutes, for Nate had disposed of the towel and held a
blue knit shirt in one hand.

He indicated a chair at the kitchen table in wordless invitation. "What was it this time? Bushels of green beans?"

Maura remained standing as she tried to look at the floor,
the ceiling or her fingers gripping the back of the chair in
front of her—anywhere but at Nate as he thrust his hands
through the arm holes of the shirt, gathered it at the nape
and raked it back over his head. The action accentuated
every muscle in his naked torso.

"Would you believe pecks of sweet peas?" she countered rather than admit she'd been blithely redecorating his
kitchen. And gawking at his physique again.

His head poked through the neck of the shirt, his eyes
mildly skeptical. "If you say so." He tugged the shirt down,
leaving it untucked. It matched his eyes exactly and brought
out their color in a vivid contrast to the relatively neutral
surroundings. Though casual, it was a stylish shirt, not what
she would have thought a man would don for a relaxed evening at home.

Perhaps he has a date. Maura flushed at her presumptuousness. She should have called before showing up at his
door.

"Well, I should be going," she said abruptly. "I didn't
mean to stay, just wanted to thank you again for your help."
She gave a short nod toward the casserole dish, avoiding his

eyes. "The stew will keep, you know, if you've something else planned for the evening."

"But I don't have anything planned," Nate said.

She glanced up. "No?" She felt strangely relieved by his assertion.

"Not a thing." Again he gestured to the chair in front of her in an invitation to sit. "In fact, if you don't have other plans yourself, would you like to have supper with me?"

The formality of his request was not lost on her. No, he didn't have a date, but he was making one right now.

He's looking for a wife, cautioned that voice in her head.

Really, Maura thought impatiently, she would never have guessed her subconscious would dredge up a years-old comment, made by a protective father, in interpretation of Nate's motives now. He was just being friendly, as she was in bringing him the casserole.

On that reflection, she found herself responding with true regret. "I'd love to, Nate, but I intended only to drop off the stew. Davey and Doreen are waiting for me at home."

"I see." He scratched his eyebrow. "And if it weren't for them, you'd stay?"

Her mouth curved upward. "This is a wonderful stew, if I do say so myself."

Out came his smile, a slow one. *Ah, there it is. You can leave now.*

But Nate had other ideas. "Then why not call them?" he suggested.

"Call them?"

"Doreen and Davey. They wouldn't mind if you ate here tonight, would they?"

"I, uh, I'm not sure," Maura stammered, taken by surprise. She hadn't expected him to pursue the matter. "I didn't plan to stay."

"Well, it won't hurt anything to ask if you can, will it?" Nate said reasonably.

"I guess not," she murmured as she watched him, without taking a step, reach for the phone hanging on the wall near the end of the counter.

"What's your number?"

Maura gave it to him. He dialed and handed her the phone.

She took it with faint trepidation. Of course Doreen would watch Davey for a few hours more, but that wasn't the point. She had a vivid image of her mother-in-law's expression when Maura had first told her of Nate's kindness. Her own uneasiness, which surely had been visible to the older woman, came back in force.

"Hello, Doreen?" she said a moment later. "It's me."

"Maura? What is it, dear? Did you forget something?"

"No. I'm still here."

"You mean at Nate's?"

"Yes." She held the receiver with both hands, very aware of Nate's eyes on her, of the puzzlement in her mother-in-law's voice. Would Doreen think she'd deliberately engineered this situation? Would Nate?

Had she?

Realizing it was too late for such analyzing, Maura took a deep breath. "Listen, Doreen," she plunged in, "Nate was wondering if I could stay for supper."

"What?" Doreen asked, then muffled the receiver. Lord, would she have to repeat it? Maura wondered. Then Doreen said, "Wait a minute. Davey wants to talk to you."

"Oh. All right," Maura assented, slightly relieved and dismayed at the same time. And still very aware of Nate's gaze. "Put him on."

"Hi, Mama. Did you tell Nate about my nickel?"

"No, honey, I haven't had a chance."

"Can I tell him?"

"Tell Nate?" She looked up. Nate raised his eyebrows. The situation seemed skewed—as if she and Nate were parents calling home to check on a child who wanted his turn at talking to both of them. Nonplussed, Maura answered,

"Sure, I guess so." She waved the receiver toward Nate. "Davey wants to talk to you."

He took the phone as she finally sank into a chair, her knees unexpectedly weak.

"Hi, pardner," Nate said easily. "Oh, that wasn't an arrowhead you found the other day? But you found an Indian-head nickel—in the garden.. ? I should say so.... No, your mom's having supper with me." Nate listened, and Maura saw that delicate change in his expression as he talked to the boy. "All right, I will. Can I talk to your grandma a minute?"

He caught her eye and gave her an *Is it okay if I do this?* lift of his shoulders. Maura nodded, unable to think of anything else to do at that point.

"Say, Doreen," Nate said in a tone that was much more easygoing than she'd ever heard from him, "would it be a big inconvenience if I kept Maura here for a while?" He smiled into the receiver, and Maura wondered if his smile was as captivating through a telephone wire as it was in person. "I mean, you do know your way around a kitchen, don't you.. ? She did? Well, then you're all set."

His voice was friendly, matter-of-fact, as if it were the most natural thing in the world for her to join him tonight. And Maura realized he was handling this matter so much better than she could have. Once again he'd sensed her dilemma and come to her rescue.

Then her premonition of the other day sprang to her mind: here was a man who could likely get anything he really wanted.

In his own time, in his own way.

A curl of damp hair brushed his forehead. He had settled one fist under the arm that held the telephone. The pose only emphasized their musculature. Gazing at him, Maura felt an overwhelming desire to find within the circle of those arms a...a freedom, an ability, if only temporarily, to share her burdens as she'd not felt she could in two years.

"Tell them I'll be home in an hour or so," she said, giving in to the inevitability of the moment.

Nate relayed her instructions and said goodbye. He turned back to her after replacing the receiver. "I hope I wasn't out of line there, Maura."

"No," she said, shaking her head. "No, I think you handled the situation beautifully. Really. I was just feeling a little . . . uncomfortable for a moment, that's all."

"And now?"

The question seemed a surface one, but Maura sensed an inquiry there that ran more deeply. She tilted her head, considering him. When he acted like this, open and just a bit vulnerable, she felt so much more at ease with him. It was more like Wayne had been—except Wayne would never have recognized her hesitations quite so clearly nor allayed them quite so deftly as Nate had.

"Now," she answered, "I'm on to you."

"You are?"

"Yes. I never knew the quiet Nate Farrell was such a smooth talker," she said glibly. "It makes me wonder what else you're hiding behind that solemn exterior."

The second she uttered the words, she wanted to take them back. An eyebrow lifted, then his smile grew in prolonged increments. Did she need any other confirmation that this man was interested in her? Or that she, against whatever better judgment she may have, was making it apparent that she was interested in him?

That creeping guilt, the twinge of disloyalty, came back. *Two years, two years,* her mind chanted in an epiphany. *Too long.*

Abruptly Nate leaned the heels of his hands on the edge of the table, bending close to her. Warmth suffused his face in the form of that singularly riveting intensity of his. It radiated from him with a dangerous heat and sent a current of sensation through her as surely as if he'd touched her.

Her conscious reasoning caught up with her subconscious, and Maura realized why this man disturbed her on an instinctive level. It was because she was drawn to him on an equally intuitive basis. And when he was like *this,* she felt powerless against him. She perceived how tenuous her sense of self-reliance and hard-won peace of mind actually was. Gazing at Nate, Maura wondered what he would say or demand or do next, because she sincerely believed she'd be helpless to resist.

Her eyes widened in a nameless fear when he opened his mouth. His gaze roved over her face, and he seemed about to do or say something, but at the last instant changed his mind.

"Let's eat," he said.

Chapter Three

Nate watched Maura from the corners of his eyes as she helped him get supper on the table. She moved with the economy of a woman at home in the kitchen, even an unfamiliar one. Plates, silverware and glasses were all found with a minimum of exploration. "Iced tea or milk?" was asked, the choice executed. Salt and pepper, two paper towels in lieu of napkins and the freshly warmed stew all appeared on the table with hardly a word being spoken.

And the furrow between Maura's delicate brows grew deeper by the second.

Nate jerked a can of peas off the shelf, opened it and dumped its contents into a bowl. He jabbed a finger at the control pad of the small microwave on the counter and watched as the peas rotated obliquely on the carousel.

Durn him for a fool. A prudent man—a *smart* man—would have accepted the casserole at his door, given Maura polite thanks with a yes, he'd return the dish within a few days, and said goodbye. But not him. He'd stood there barely able to carry on a conversation as he racked his brain for a way to get her to stay. Then when he'd found one, he jumped on it like a dog on a rabbit, and hang common sense.

Who could blame him, though? Over the past thirty-six hours, his hopes had alternately risen and plunged like a roller coaster at the thought of Maura Foster. The very fact she continued to affect him that way told him he needed to get a little distance. But just when he had decided he'd read too much into her actions and that the best course was the one he'd stayed on most of his life, here she came right up to his door! She looked so pretty tonight in that crisp dress with its bits of spring color—pink and blue and yellow—that brought out the roses in her cheeks. It didn't seem to him she would have gone to such trouble if there was no more to her gesture than thanks. And when she stared and stammered and blushed, he was almost *sure* there was more.

The microwave chimed, and Nate carefully removed the heated bowl of peas and set it on the table. Maura had already taken a seat, and he slid into the chair opposite hers. The dense cloud of silence hung between them.

"Wait." Maura's voice finally broke the stillness as he reached for the large serving spoon next to the stew. "Will you... Would you like me to say grace?"

"Oh. Sure." His hand withdrew and joined his other as he watched Maura lower her eyes. In repose, her features became serene. The crease between her brows disappeared. Surrounded by the golden glow of her hair, her face seemed to take on an angelic cast. Although there was nothing heavenly in his thoughts as Nate observed the sweet curve of her lips moving in a simple prayer, a certain sense of peace settled over him.

When finished with her short thanksgiving, she glanced up and smiled at him, the tranquil mood lingering between them. Nate smiled back, glad they seemed to have gotten past the awkward moment. If only they could maintain the comfortable atmosphere.

He passed her the peas. "How's the garden coming?" he asked on a subject that seemed suitably conversational.

"Fully planted."

"What did you put in?"

"A mixture of determinate tomatoes for canning and indeterminate for eating. Bush beans, pole beans, onion sets, peppers, carrots—" she ticked them off "—and, let's see...beets—much to Davey's despair—zucchini and, to make up for the beets, a few pumpkin vines."

"Sounds like you'll be able to hold your head up as the town's Master Gardener."

"Yes." She lightly salted her food. "Actually I was joking about that aspect the other day. I need a large vegetable garden. It makes it easier to get by."

"*Are* you able to get by, Maura?" he asked, not caring if it sounded as if he pried. He needed to know she was doing all right.

She nodded. "I don't mind telling you we had a rough six months there. I was about ready to take a secretarial job in Newton last summer when the operation on Davey's crossed eye came up. I couldn't bear the thought of being away from him over ten hours a day at a time I felt he needed me most. I hoped something in Soldier Creek would turn up eventually, and it just about killed me to see our savings dwindling as the months went by."

Nate felt a twinge of remorse. "Things probably wouldn't have been so tight if my parents' inn...if it hadn't..."

"Yes, it's a shame that tornado leveled their home and deprived me of a job." He gave her a sharp glance and noted the irony in her eye. He frowned ruefully. "You know what I mean."

She took a bite of stew and chewed thoughtfully. "Yes, I know. I would have loved to help your family run their inn, but you see, everything's worked out for the best. Your parents have rebuilt and are running the inn just fine with Callie's help. She's married Drew and come back to live right next to them. And I have a wonderful job at the library.'' Her tone was definite, as if she wouldn't let herself consider even the possibility that the future might fail to bring all she hoped it would.

But she was right. Things were working out. Never had Nate seen his parents happier, more so than they had been when Dad was farming. And they were in hog heaven having Callie a half mile away. His sister had started her own inn at the Barnett homestead, and she and his mother had nearly carved a rut in the road as they went back and forth from their homes tens of times a week.

Yes, trust Maura to see a devastating tornado as a happy happenstance, but no denying when the dust had settled, fate had seen to it that everything and everyone had found its place. Except, perhaps, for him.

Neither of them spoke for a few moments as they ate.

"Nate," Maura said suddenly.

He looked up. "Yes?"

She lifted a forkful of stew, pausing halfway to her lips. "I was wondering why you didn't say something to me about tilling my garden the new, better way, like you're doing.''

His stomach did an odd flip. *Durn.* He didn't want to get into this subject. Not at all. He wasn't afraid or ashamed to talk about his plans, but he didn't want to emphasize his difficulties, either, not to Maura. And there was the risk that, even with an explanation, he might still seem crazy to her, and Nate had no clue how he'd handle that development.

Yet the expression in her brown eyes was just as Davey's had been when he'd studied Nate so astutely yesterday. No criticism lingered in those velvet depths. Her curiosity wasn't idle, either. She just wanted to know. And he realized he wanted her, more than anyone else, to understand.

"What I'm doing isn't necessarily better, Maura," he explained slowly. "I mean, farmers have been plowing and cultivating their fields since time began, and making a good living. But research shows it's better to leave the land be in the fall and let a protective layer of organic litter keep down the erosion that's going to happen to some extent anyway."

"So this fall, after the garden's done producing, you think I shouldn't spade it?"

"No..." Nate pushed his plate away with the edge of his thumb and unconsciously tipped his chair back to balance on its back legs, a pose he thought best in. With a quick glance at Maura, he realized this might not be considered strictly polite and let the front legs drift to the floor again as inconspicuously as possible. "You place different demands on the soil when you garden. You're looking for a higher yield, and in such a limited space you've got more ways to protect the soil's properties. You can mulch to hold in moisture and discourage weeds. You can build a berm around the garden to prevent runoff. And in the fall, you *want* to till so you get the pests out into the air where the cold will destroy them and the birds can eat them. You want that opportunity to work in organic matter like fallen leaves and your compost. On a farmwide scale, though, I'm working with the lesser of two evils, because the more a farmer plows, the more wind and water erosion he causes."

Again he'd liked to have dropped the subject, but he could see her puzzling. "So you still plow in the spring, but somehow differently?" she asked.

Nate nodded, shifting in his chair under her searching gaze. This was getting into the really radical changes in his farming. "I use a piece of equipment called a ridge tiller that scoops mounds of dirt into hills and valleys. I plant on the ridge—the hill, that is—so that when I treat the crop, I don't use as much herbicide or pesticide. Better for the land, in addition to saving money and time. In fact, my aim is to get to the point where I don't use any chemical pest controllers at all on the soil. The trade-off is that I'll have to cultivate more often throughout the growing season."

He hesitated, unsure of how much she wanted to know or how much he wanted to reveal. Ridge tilling in and of itself was a novel-enough undertaking in central Iowa without his introducing the whole organic concept—not to mention his plans for letting parts of the farm return to marsh! No, he'd be better off if he didn't get into that area of discussion.

But then Maura laid one forearm over the other on the table and leaned forward in a sincere interest that satisfied something within Nate Farrell that had gone long unfulfilled. It hit him hard, right in the gut, and he found himself needing to go on.

"I'm trying some alternative crops, like canola and amaranth, that place different demands on the soil and discourage the pests that would go for a crop that had been planted there before."

"I know a little about that," Maura interrupted. "I learned about integrated pest management in my Master Gardener courses. You try to control pests culturally and mechanically, as well as chemically."

Nate blinked in pleased amazement. "Exactly. But you know and I know that most farmers in these parts look for the fastest and most efficient way of getting the greatest yield from their land." He shrugged. "I'll allow it's fast, but it isn't efficient. Rotating your crops and fertilizing naturally, combined with some of the old standbys like planting with the contour of the land to keep erosion down, doesn't sap the soil's properties so much and lets it start to return to a more balanced, natural state."

"But what about your yields?" Maura asked. "Isn't it risky to grow something there isn't as big a market for, or grow less of it? How can you make a profit?"

"Sure, it's a risk. I had to buy a special ridge tiller, and I have to find alternative markets, ones that pay more because it does cost more to produce organically grown crops. But the key is diversifying—if one crop is hit hard by a blight or pest that winters over, I still have other crops that will come in at their usual yield. And weighed against the amount of money I'd have to put out not only to buy but also broadcast herbicides, insecticides and fertilizers, it's not a great loss. Timewise, I come out ahead by ridge tilling and rotating crops, since I don't have to prepare the soil in other ways. I can devote time to raising some beef cattle and feeder pigs that provide a natural fertilizer while cashing in on the growing market for contamination-free stock."

Absently Nate fingered the edge of his napkin. "Profit aside, though, I'm just trying to take away as little as possible from the land, partly so I won't have to spend time and money putting it back, but mostly because it's . . . right."

"I see." Maura's gaze shifted sightlessly as she considered his comments. Again he felt that sense of completion. Maura seemed to accept his right to farm as he wanted to. He hoped his explanations had been clear, for he wanted her understanding, too.

Never did he wish for something more, except with her. All his life he'd found the means to happiness within his own being. He'd never wanted for anything: a sense of purpose, the love and approbation of his family. Or if he had wanted something, he'd possessed the patience to let it come to him as it would, much as he'd waited for his father to turn the farm over to him, allowing him to begin what he saw as doing right by the land.

"I wonder why I wasn't taught some of these alternatives in my Master Gardener classes," Maura said musingly. "I mean, I've learned how to control insects, diseases and weeds more naturally, but you'd think the university would teach organic methods if they could."

"Surely you've at least heard of some of these techniques before now, know a little bit about them."

"Oh, I've heard." Maura pushed a few peas around on her plate with her fork. She hesitated, then looked up at him again. "But a lot of people reject them out of hand. I mean, the farmers don't mind calling on the extension service for updates on outbreaks of pests or how the corn's doing statewide, but they aren't about to have the university telling them what they should be planting or how they should be plowing when, like you said, the farmers have been making a living doing it the same way for years."

He chuckled at her accurate assessment of the prevailing attitude. "I think the only way some farmers would ever change is if they had hard evidence that their yields would improve. But probably the reason you weren't taught different methods is because you'll be talking to people about their personal gardens. Like I said, you're placing different demands on the soil. And your audience is limited to other gardeners, not the farmers the university hasn't been able to convince for years. There's no good reason for the university to make you take that kind of heat."

"Yet you've put your reputation on the line for them," she murmured.

"I put it on the line for myself," he corrected, "because I believe I can make a difference."

Yes, he felt a definite consolation being able to discuss this subject with Maura. He was being given a chance to explain the significance of this undertaking. And she did seem to understand, so much more than anyone else ever had—not his father, who supported his efforts while still finding them puzzling in their newfangledness; not his mother or sister or even his friend Drew, who didn't have the same sort of connection with the land that he had.

Or, it struck him, that Maura had.

Nate glanced up and caught her steady brown-eyed gaze on him. "Yes, you believe in something different," she said. "You've been paying a price for that, haven't you, Nate?"

He paused. The conversation could end here, but now that he'd known the gift of her understanding, he wanted even more. "To the people of Soldier Creek, I'm Crazy Nate," he said with a shake of his head. "And maybe in a way I *am* crazy. Crazy for exposing my family, especially Dad, to criticism for my actions, not theirs. The reason I waited until Dad turned the farm over to me was because I could never've asked him to do anything he didn't support one hundred percent."

She caught her breath softly at his words, and he felt her empathy. "I didn't know your father was being held up to criticism," she said.

"It surprises me, too. But it figures, in a way. Most of the remarks have come from men like my dad, who've been farming since the fifties. The farmers more my age—well, they've pretty well kept mum, I guess to see if Nate Farrell ruins his land first before making any drastic changes themselves. And really, I don't mind being a guinea pig. But when I hear about the old codgers in town wondering how Oran Farrell could raise such a son... that's when I can't ignore it."

Through the screen door came the intermittent bang of feeders, the occasional lowing of a cow, sounds that had seeped into his being over the years and become a part of him as surely as his own heartbeat. This time when his chair tipped backward, almost of its own volition, Nate let it and balanced himself on two legs. "You know, when I took Davey to Ernie's the other day, I couldn't help thinking Dad should have been there, shooting the breeze with those guys. He deserves that sort of relaxation, after everything he's been through in the last few years. A heart condition that robbed his ability to farm his land, losing his family home to a tornado. But Dad told me a few months ago he didn't find the company at Ernie's or the café that enlivening anymore."

Nate studied his hands, fingers laced against his stomach, his thumbs making slow circles around each other. "I'd kind of hoped the ruckus would die down after a while, but I guess nothing else has come up to beat 'Farrell's Folly.' Unfortunately it'll take a few years for me to prove I'm not off my nut. Until then, though... I can't help but worry about Dad."

Nate continued to stare at his hands and wondered if he'd said too much. He'd never put much stock in explanations, mainly because they sounded so often like excuses, as if he needed to convince himself more than others of the validity of his actions and ideals. In his mind, it was better, most of the time, to go along, showing by those actions instead of by words the kind of man he was.

And yet it felt so right to talk to Maura this way.

"Nate."

He looked up.

"People would understand if they knew," she said.

He pressed his lips together and nodded. "I suppose so. At least if they knew I'd studied these methods for years," he said. "I mean, I grew up in this community, ran around with these men's sons, dated their daughters. You'd think they'd know I'm not crazy."

Maura rolled her eyes in commiseration. "I've often wondered what the cutoff age is for being able to act unconventional without everybody and their brother talking about it," she said with a straight face.

He cocked a one-sided smile at her. " 'If you change it, they will gossip,' " he quipped.

They laughed.

"Kevin Costner I'm not," Nate said without rancor, glad for the change of subject. He was a little embarrassed for having run off at the mouth for so long in a way that was most unlike him, but he savored the closeness it had produced between them. "I hear the voice of experience, though. I'm curious what you do that might be considered even a tad unconventional."

She colored slightly. "I talk to myself," she confessed.

"I hate to break it to you, but quite a few people do that."

"I mean I *talk*. Out loud." She waved one hand back and forth before settling it over her opposite shoulder. "I talk to my flowers, to my vegetable garden."

"The individual vegetables or in congregation? There's a difference, you know."

She chuckled. "Both. Every once in a while it strikes me how odd I must seem, and I picture old Mrs. Connelly. You know, she wore that bright red wig, and you never saw her without two big circles of rouge on her wrinkled cheeks. I remember how, when I was a girl, I used to pass her on the street—you could hear her coming from a block away—and she'd be talking a mile a minute. Pass you right by without even noticing you.''

"I think you're safe as long as you confine your one-sided conversations to your own backyard," Nate absolved her. "But I'll let you know when I can hear you all the way out here.''

Maura laughed again. "Thank you. I feel so much better.'' The mirth left her face suddenly as she ducked her head and studied her hand as it rubbed back and forth across her arm. "I... Sometimes I talk to Wayne," she said. She peered at him, her brown eyes watchful from beneath her lashes.

Instead of withdrawing, as was his first impulse at the mention of her husband, Nate made sure his eyes contained all the empathy he felt for her and her own concerns. "What do you talk about?" he asked.

"Oh, Davey mostly." Her gaze drifted away from his. "It helps to think he might be listening to me from somewhere. I mean, I find it easier to accept that a twenty-eight-year-old man could be here one day and gone the next if I can believe I still have some way to let him know how we're doing. Part of it's habit." She paused, her expression reflective. "And part, I suppose, is a kind of selfish compulsion to remember." She stopped, as if disturbed by her admission.

"How's that, Maura?" he prompted softly.

She pressed the back of her fingers to her lips before her hand fell away. "Sometimes I can't help thinking, what if it had been me?" Abruptly she fixed him with a look of such anguish a lump formed in his throat. "What if I'd died and left a husband and three-year-old child behind? I'd want to be remembered, because it breaks my heart to even consider that... to think that my son might forget the mother who loved him for so short a time.''

Maura dropped her gaze once again, but not before Nate caught the glistening in her eyes. His throat grew ever tighter in pain for her suffering, even while his own heart sank.

Just as she had given it to him, he realized she was asking for acceptance if not an understanding of her circumstances. And her choices. The problem was Nate did understand. Had Davey been his own, he would want the boy to remember. And, perverse as it seemed, had he been Maura's husband, he would want her to remember, too, for forever. Maura was the kind of woman who loved greatly and deeply. That was one of the qualities that drew him to her. But Maura had greatly loved Wayne Foster. And there was room for only one man in her heart.

So it wasn't so simple a matter as waiting for her to get over Wayne. Disappointment rose in Nate, stronger and more real than he would imagine it could have been at this stage. He shouldn't have entertained even the slimmest of hopes—but he had. He would have liked a chance. Just one chance.

Her sweet mouth was rigid with suppressed emotion, her eyes downcast. Nate couldn't have stopped his arm from reaching across the table to lay its hand over hers. Her fingers quivered beneath his palm.

"Maura," he said quietly. He squeezed her hand. "I understand. You know that, don't you?"

She kept her head bent. "Do you?" she whispered.

"Maura."

She lifted her chin then, and he saw her fear. She *was* afraid of him! And God, it cut him.

Why? For some reason, she was frightened by what she saw in his eyes. He knew he'd frightened her years ago, but what had he done since to bring that cornered, threatened look to her face? Yesterday he might have thought she saw Crazy Nate and his reputation as the danger to her and her son and their new life together. But not after their conversation just now. Maura didn't hold his farming against him.

She understood and accepted his reasons for taking the risks he did.

So what was it?

With tremendous effort, Nate managed to school his features, though his thoughts whirled with the turbulence of a tornado. Actually he'd lied—he didn't understand. If she still loved Wayne so greatly, then how could Nate threaten her? Something else wasn't right, either, because the sparks were there between them, as were the threads of a deep and satisfying accord.

But in her eyes they could flame no brighter, grow no stronger. What she was saying was that she'd made her choice—years ago and now. And nothing had changed.

He had little choice but to comply with her wishes.

It wouldn't be easy, he realized. It hadn't been easy to back off before, but for some reason this time it would be infinitely more difficult. He'd rather have taken Wayne Foster on again in the flesh, because he knew of no way to fight a dead man.

The thought spurred the memory of that day when he and Wayne Foster had set into action the course of events that would influence their young lives for many a year after. He shook his head. *If only I'd known.* If only he'd known... then what? What would he have done differently?

The kitchen closed in on him of a sudden. Not that it shrank around him, but it seemed as if he became larger, ready to burst. He knew it as a familiar and much too dangerous feeling.

Nate rose abruptly, raking a restless hand through his hair. "How about taking a walk?" he asked. They both needed a few moments to collect themselves.

Maura nodded and preceded him to the door. Once outside, Nate took a lung-filling breath, letting it out slowly. He felt better instantly.

The sun hung low in the sky, bathing them in a mellow warmth that staved off the chill of the mild May evening. In silent agreement, they walked toward the edge of the large yard and stopped by the low fence that separated the lawn from the newly planted land. Nate rested his forearms on the split-rail fence and found a measure of peace, as he always did, in contemplating his handiwork.

He had chosen this field as the first in which to implement his new methods. Though, if he'd been a smarter man—and Nate was coming around to the suspicion that he might not be—he'd have chosen a field off the road where he'd be spared every Tom, Dick and Harry driving by and wondering what on God's green earth Crazy Nate was up to. But he'd wanted the ability to do just this, to walk out here of an evening and simply... look at it.

"What are you thinking, Nate?" Maura asked softly. He glanced at her in the golden light. Her face was once again composed, chestnut brown eyes showing gentle concern. Had it been so obvious what he'd wanted?

Seeking distance, Nate turned back to inspecting the field. Barely a few inches tall, the bean shoots pushed stalwartly out of the black earth. From this angle, with the evening sun creating long shadows, it was even easier to see the height and depth of the ridges. They seemed to undulate like eddying water over the gently rolling land in a way that Nate found more satisfying than observing his fields had ever been.

He recalled the question Maura had put to him. She had listened to, understood and accepted his choices. Could he offer her any less?

"I've been thinking about Wayne, that fight we got into," he answered. "I was wishing it had never happened. Even though we were eventually able to shake hands and let bygones go by, neither of us ever forgot. We were never easy in each other's company after that, and it's a shame because Wayne was a good man."

That said, he shut his mouth firmly, eyes straight ahead. He'd say no more on the subject. He wanted her to know there were no hard feelings, but she didn't need him dredging up more painful memories of Wayne. He didn't think he could stand to see that look of misery enter her eyes again.

"He was a good man," Maura agreed in a soft voice, "but he should never have come at you that night, no matter what his reasons were."

Nate shot her a probing glance. She gave him an opening, and he saw another chance to explain himself, this time for events that had long ago passed under the bridge but that she had a right to have explained to her. "I'd never have asked you out, you know, if I'd half a notion you two were going steady."

"We weren't." Maura turned and leaned back against the fence, hands wrapped around her elbows. "I mean, we were dating, but my father didn't want me going steady until I graduated high school, a whole year from then. To be fair, though, there *was* an...understanding between Wayne and me. It was all very innocent, and without saying so, we knew there was plenty of time for declarations. The other boys our age knew, and they didn't ask me out. That's what worried Dad—that I would become serious about Wayne simply because no other option would present itself. Or himself." She cast him a dry look. "Then the older and worldly-wise Nate Farrell asked me out."

Nate nodded, remembering. He'd been out of the loop, having spent the two years since his own graduation taking classes in agribusiness at the area community college while still helping his father farm. Once he got the opportunity to catch his breath, he'd noticed Maura Bishop immediately. He'd seen instantly that she was different, in the way she moved, in the way she smiled, which made her chirpy, twittery friends inordinately less fascinating. Her thoughtful serenity had radiated like an aura around her even then and had reached out and touched him as it must have touched Wayne Foster.

Nate had gone out with girls before but he knew this one was special, could be special for a long, long time. He asked her out, almost fearful that she would turn out to be less than he imagined. Yet when she'd answered his knock on her door that mellow spring evening more than a decade ago and she had looked up at him with brown eyes shy but filled with inherent kindness, he'd known for certain that Maura Bishop was going to affect him in a big way. And then, from behind her, he'd seen Don Bishop rise from his easy chair, his face less welcoming.

"I got the impression, though, your dad didn't think I was an appropriate diversion," Nate said. "Even before what happened later."

"No..." Maura drew the word out, flushing. "He almost didn't let me leave the house. He thought Wayne would be picking me up that evening, and it wasn't until right before you arrived that it came out I was going out with—" she lowered her voice to a scandalized whisper "—*an older man.* I didn't know he considered you off-limits."

Nate shook his head, truly puzzled. "Because I was a few years older?"

She grew even pinker, stammered a bit, then seemed to make the decision to come clean. "Actually it was because, Dad said, you were looking for a wife," she blurted out. "I know that must sound ridiculous now, seeing as you haven't...aren't—" She took a deep breath and faced him squarely. "He said since you were done with your schooling and had a place of your own... Everyone knew you were going to farm for a living. It just seemed like a logical conclusion to my father, and he knew how I was—shy and liable to take things too seriously. He didn't want me getting in over my head."

"Well, you can't blame parents for doing what they think is right," Nate admitted. When it came right down to it, Don Bishop had been correct in his assessment, in a way. It wasn't as if there'd been a slot in Nate's life he wanted to fill and had been taking a bead on the likely candidates. It was more as if Maura had appeared, and suddenly a place in his life opened up for her. "If he felt that way, it's hard to believe he let you go out with me even once," he said.

"He did only because I put my foot down," she answered. Nate had a hard time imagining Maura at any age, let alone seventeen, putting her foot down. "I told him it would be rude to cancel the date on the doorstep. And it wasn't like you were going to elope with me that very night."

"No," he allowed. His state of mind had nearly been that volatile, though. He'd been uncharacteristically impulsive, falling for her like a ton of bricks. The evening had been one of discovery. He'd decided to skip the movie and go straight to the Newton Pizza Hut, where they'd been oblivious to the usual Friday-night crowd as they talked. Mostly they'd sat in a comfortable and strangely gratifying silence—as if the communication between them went much deeper than words.

Knowing now what Don Bishop had thought of him, what thoughts Maura's head had been filled with, Nate saw the evening in a whole different light. Perhaps the sense of connection had been on his side alone. "Did *you* think I was looking for a wife, Maura?"

She broke eye contact again, her teeth tugging at her lower lip. "I didn't at first. I thought you were very nice, and we were having a good time. But later..."

Later Nate had taken Maura home. He'd escorted her to her door with his feet barely touching the sidewalk. Vividly he remembered to this day how, when he turned her to him, an echo of his own intense feelings filled her eyes, though less certain, more tentative. That hadn't bothered him; he'd known even then she was the kind who gave her love with care. With all the ardor of youth, though, he had wanted to experience that first rush of love to the fullest, wanted to show her how he felt.

"Can I kiss you good-night?" he had whispered.

The rounding of her eyes had spoken her apprehension, yet in their brown depths he saw the effect of his own gaze. She'd nodded as if under a spell, and he'd lifted her chin with one hand, drawing her close with the other as he bent his face to hers.

Nate had paused, wrought with anticipation but wanting to prolong the experience of that first kiss, wanting to see her response to his touch, which would tell him exactly how she felt about him. Her lashes had fluttered down a second before, but at his hesitation, she opened her eyes again. Gone was the apprehension. There was only an acknowledgment—and a welcoming—of that spell weaving its way around her, around them.

And in those few moments, staring into Maura's eyes, Nate had felt the exhilaration of holding in his hands the always elusive future. Never since had he felt that certainty that comes from not merely knowing what one wants from life, but knowing it is within one's grasp.

Then her attention had flickered to something behind him. He had turned, and there stood a wild-eyed Wayne Foster, frozen in disbelief. In fear.

Nate tore his mind's eye from the graphic memory that made the closed-in feeling return. His gaze fell naturally to the ground, and he stooped to pick a wild violet at his feet. Brushing his fingertips against the soft petals, he said, "You know, I could tell the instant I saw Wayne I was in for a fight."

"Yes, well . . . he was scared, you see," Maura said, as if she wanted this opportunity to explain, too. Or defend. "I'd told him I had a date with someone else and, though he wasn't happy about it, he seemed to accept it. Until he found out it was you."

"Me? Why would I be different from another guy?"

"Wayne was afraid he couldn't compete, Nate. You were twenty, more experienced, with your own car and your own place," she said. "I'm not excusing Wayne's actions, but he was crazy with panic that I'd choose you over him, and his fear drove him to lash out at you."

Lashing out didn't begin to describe what Wayne did, Nate thought. Without warning, the seventeen-year-old had attacked him. Wayne had fought like a dervish, his arms whirling windmills that mostly failed to make contact. Nate had raised his own arms in defense and, seeing the shock on Maura's face, wondered madly how to salvage the situation while not losing any teeth. While not losing her.

"Believe me, Maura," he went on, halfway lost in the past, "I tried to block the blows without throwing any punches myself, but he wouldn't let up. He just kept coming and coming. And then..."

Then Maura had cried out.

"Wayne!" she'd screamed. Not "Nate!" Not even "Stop it, both of you!" With that cry, something in Nate had snapped. His own frustration had boiled over into a kind of fury, though he was still uncertain why. Perhaps it had been because he realized his tunnel vision had kept him from considering Maura might have other boyfriends. Perhaps it was injured pride at the prospect of losing a girl to a seventeen-year-old when moments before he'd felt he held her love in his hand. Or perhaps it had been his own youth-intensified emotions, knowing he'd let his passions run away with him and override the careful reasoning that was more like him.

It'd been none of those reasons, Nate realized now. What he'd felt then, what he felt now, was the frustration of getting not even a chance to explore the possibilities he'd glimpsed in Maura's eyes.

In any case, he'd pulled back his arm and delivered a punishing blow, calculated to injure, to Wayne Foster's face. Cartilage had split beneath his knuckles. Wayne had sunk to his knees, gasping for breath and holding his nose as blood seeped between his fingers.

Through a red haze, Nate had heard the pounding of feet from within Maura's house. The door crashed open and Don Bishop had taken in the scene in a glance before turning to Maura, clearly expecting her to indicate which boy was culpable. Maura had seemed to be held immobile in a trap of indecision, and tenuous hope had sprung up in Nate.

Then she'd moved forward and knelt at Wayne's side.

"I had to choose, Nate," she said now, with uncanny insight into his thoughts. "I didn't think it was fair that I had to, but I realized that if the strength of your feelings—both yours and Wayne's—had brought you to that point, neither of you would have accepted anything but a clear-cut choice."

"We *were* quite a pair of pups, weren't we?" he said, forcing a lightness into his voice he didn't feel. "Everything's so life-or-death when you're that age." What he didn't ask was *Why Wayne? Why not me?*

Again, though, Maura seemed to guess his thoughts. "I knew Wayne, you see, knew him and understood him. I've always been able to understand him." And what she didn't say was that she had not understood Nate Farrell and did not understand him now.

But she could. She had, just a few moments earlier, when he'd spoken about his farming and his father.

Nate tossed away the delicate violet, already wilting from the warmth of his fingers. Again he hadn't intended the explanation to go into such depth, though Maura had seemed to need to justify her actions that day, too. He wondered why. He knew why he had, though it was all ancient history that no one could change with any amount of explaining. Even without Wayne's confrontation, Maura's father would never have let her go out with Nate again, at least not for a few years.

Still, Nate would have liked that opportunity.

"Well." He blew out a gust of air. "I'm glad we talked about what happened. You know, a person can't avoid leaving a few loose ends hanging as he goes through life, but that was one loose end I could have tied up years ago and didn't."

"I've felt the same. I realized the other day that I'd practically forgotten what happened—or blocked it from my mind, though I can't imagine why. Maybe because I never talked it out with anyone."

"Not even with Wayne?" he asked.

"Believe it or not, we never spoke a word about it between us. I tried to bring it up a few times, wanting to explore what it meant to our relationship. He wouldn't discuss it, even after we were married, and I always felt it there, between us—not in a critical way, but still...I don't know." Maura absently brushed the end of her braid against her cheek in a way that made Nate swallow and avert his gaze. Automatically he squatted and reached between the rails to pull up a tiny chickweed growing next to the fence post. "Maybe he knew he hadn't acted all that admirably and didn't want to dwell on it, but I had some bad feelings I needed to deal with. I thought bringing it out in the open would help me let go of them. But every time, Wayne clammed up. I think he was always a little bit...afraid, for some reason. Afraid he might still lose me."

That brought his head up. *Ah-ha,* Nate thought, catching his upper lip in his teeth to keep from saying anything. He wondered if Maura knew what she'd just admitted about Wayne, herself and their marriage. Even her reasons for preserving her husband's memory.

Or her reasons for being afraid of Nate. Thinking back over their conversation and her reactions, he felt he stumbled onto a very important possibility: maybe things hadn't been so perfect between Maura and Wayne. He had no doubt she'd loved her husband, but maybe Wayne had realized he'd come close to losing her not because he lacked a few years of maturity, but because something was missing between them—something that made the difference between a good relationship and a once-in-a-lifetime relationship. Perhaps he'd been afraid that, had she the opportunity to find that elusive something somewhere else, she would have recognized it and no longer would she love Wayne Foster.

Of course, he could be way off base, but where a moment ago he'd seen a door close, Nate now saw another one open, a sliver of opportunity splitting the darkness. It was a small opening, but an opening nonetheless. It was a chance.

"Well," Maura said in a bright change of tone, as if she did indeed realize the implications of her last statement. With a sudden movement, she pushed away from the fence. "I need to get on home."

Nate rose. "I hope Davey hasn't run Doreen ragged."

"I'd be surprised if he has. No, Davey's a different kind of handful. Unless you actually meant . . . He was good for you the other day, wasn't he, Nate?" she asked. "I forgot to ask you when you brought him home."

"Davey was fine," he assured her. He saw no reason to rehash the situation they'd encountered at Ernie's. Although, if Davey asked, Nate would have liked the opportunity to tell the boy in his own words what the remarks made by Arvid and his gang meant, and about the circumstances between him and Wayne. But Nate had an inkling Davey was one person who needed no explanation. "Did he tell you anything?"

"Oh, he gave me a short rundown." They started toward her car. "I think he would have said more but felt I really wouldn't understand the significance of the experience. Not the woman who almost took him to a beauty parlor. But I want you to tell me something," she said, stopping abruptly.

He turned and regarded her. "Yes?"

"When did you learn to talk to little boys?" she asked almost suspiciously, even a little defensively.

"When did you?" he countered.

A corner of her mouth dented her cheek, just as Davey's had. "When I had one," she answered as she started toward him. "Although I'll admit to limited success in that area."

"That's because it's not a matter of talking to them, it's a matter of learning to think like them."

"Really? And when did you learn to think like a little boy?"

"When I was one," Nate said sagely.

Maura burst out laughing. "If that's what it takes, then I'm doomed," she groaned.

"Davey can't be *that* much of a handful." The warmth of a small hand in his returned as Nate thought of the boy. "I mean, I see some of these rapscallions running around. I'm not one to lay a hand on a child, but there're a few kids around town I wouldn't mind taking a lick to."

"If only he were a little more rambunctious," Maura said. The worry line appeared, a deep groove, and Nate suppressed a strong urge to smooth it away. "I'd know how to handle that kind of behavior."

He wanted to help her, but for all his pearls of wisdom, he knew very little about children. Again he found himself remembering that small, serious face and those perceptive brown eyes. He'd like to help Davey, almost as much as he'd like to help Maura.

"You might look into some physical activities for Davey," he suggested. "Red Cross swimming lessons will be starting after the Newton pool opens in June. Or there's Scouts. Or—" He shrugged apologetically, as much in the dark as she was, and he felt for some reason he was letting her down. "Shoot, I don't know. I'm no expert. Maybe it's just a matter of giving you both some time to find your way."

They had reached her car, and Maura turned to him. "You're probably right. It's just that lately I've felt like Rip Van Winkle or something. After two years, I'm finally waking up and everything's changed."

A lock of flaxen hair had come loose from her braid and blew across her cheek. This time Nate gave in to his impulse to touch her and reached out to brush it back just as she raised her hand to do so. Her fingers inadvertently trapped his against her temple. They both froze, eyes locked, for just an instant before he slid his hand backward on her smooth skin, her palm still covering his, and tucked the strands behind her ear.

"Maybe it's you who's changed, Maura," he said softly.

Her reaction was that slight widening of her eyes. Perhaps not quite fear, Nate thought, but surprise—an encouraging sign. Her hand fell away, taking his with it, then it disappeared around her side as she reached for and found the door handle. Nate held the car door open for her and closed it firmly after she had slid into her seat. She looked up at him with those wide brown eyes, then she smiled, as if doing so would banish her troubles and doubts. "Thanks, Nate, for listening."

"Me, too. Thanks, I mean. For dinner and everything."

"I enjoyed learning about your new farming techniques. I hope they succeed." She made it sound as if it would be a long time before they'd see each other again.

Not if I can help it. He ignored her implication and gave her a quick nod of acknowledgment. "Time will tell, I expect."

She started the car and sat staring out the windshield for a moment while the engine's idle evened out. Then she gave him another smile, soft and warm. "You're a good man, too, Nate Farrell," she said through the half-open window. "Don't let anyone ever try to tell you different."

Nate said nothing as she put the car in reverse and backed out of the drive and onto the road. He plucked a rock from the grass and lifted it, ready to pitch it onto the gravel drive. He hesitated, though. He did a lot of that: looked to his land for distraction, for confirmation, for solace. For understanding.

But now there was Maura's understanding, strong and true. And then it hit him: Maura had understood Wayne, understood his hopes, *his* fears, in a way that, with her capacity for compassion and empathy, she couldn't prevent herself from responding to. If she didn't understand Nate, how could he ever expect her to respond to him?

He didn't want her compassion, though; he wanted her love. And he could win it, he realized, if he would open up to her.

Nate tossed the rough stone lightly in his hand. Davey wasn't the only one who needed to come out of his shell. They had a lot to learn. Davey, him—and Maura.

Sliding the stone into position between his thumb and first two fingers, he cocked his arm. The stone arced across the dusky sky. He didn't see, didn't hear it fall to earth.

For once he didn't need to.

Chapter Four

"Mama?"

"Son?"

"What's a ru-runcible spoon?"

Maura swept a last swath of paste across the back of a manila library pocket before fixing it on the inside cover of a new book. At nearly closing time, she and Davey were the only ones in the library, Maura at her desk and Davey in the story corner on the far side of the room, hidden by shelves of books.

She permitted herself a proud smile, for herself as much as for Davey. Since she'd started working at the library, he'd become much more curious about things and more willing to ask questions, though some she found herself hard-pressed to answer. She'd decided her best course of action was to make learning a mutual activity. They'd discover the world together.

"A runcible spoon," she mused. "How's it used?"

Silence, then she heard a shuffling of pages, followed by the sound of rubber-soled feet across the linoleum as Davey trekked over to her desk. Standing beside her, he laid in front of her the illustrated book of nursery rhymes she'd been reading to her preschoolers. With a finger following the words for Davey's benefit, she read the lines from "The Owl and the Pussycat". "'They dined on mince, and slices of quince,/Which they ate with a runcible spoon.' Well, Davey boy, I don't know what a runcible spoon is. But I have an idea how we can find out. Let's look it up in the dictionary."

He propped his elbows on the edge of her desk, squinted the bridge of his glasses upward on his nose and watched as she made a production of turning to the reference section behind her and locating the dictionary.

"What letter do you suppose 'runcible' comes under? *S* or *T*?"

"*R*," Davey said soberly, not taking the bait.

"*R* it is," Maura said, finding the definition. "'A three-pronged fork...curved like a spoon and having a cutting edge.' Look, they show a picture." She angled the dictionary for him to see better.

Davey studied the drawing, blinked twice behind his glasses, and glanced up at her. "It looks like a fork."

"Well, it is, kind of." She cocked her head to one side, taking another assessment of the figure. "It's curved like a spoon—see?—even though it's got tines like a fork."

"Then why don't they call it a...*runcible* fork?" He looked surprised but pleased at getting the word out without stumbling over it. It *was* a strange word, Maura mentally rationalized.

She raised her brows apologetically. "I don't know why. And now *you* know mothers don't know everything."

"What about li-berrians?" he asked innocently, mangling her title.

"Neither do they." She leaned over and rocked her forehead against his as they snickered. Maura had always thought her son had a jolly laugh, a chortle really, low and slightly rascally, as if he got a little bit more of a joke than others did but wouldn't say what. She loved it when she was able to brighten his face—much as she'd taken pleasure in bringing out Nate's smile. It was a definite challenge in both cases. She'd heard more of Davey's laugh lately, though still not enough to alleviate the bulk of her worries about him. With that thought, she reached a hand across to squeeze the back of his neck. Her son allowed the touch for barely a second before pulling away.

"What's quince?" he asked.

"That I know," Maura said, suppressing her hurt. *He's growing up.* "It's a fruit."

"What's mince?" he continued to grill her.

"Now, you know that one. Like the mince in my mincemeat pie?"

He thought a moment. "What's a dell?"

"A dell?"

Davey turned the page to the next nursery rhyme. "Like 'The Farmer in the Dell,'" he explained.

"Oh, I see. Well, a dell is a little valley. And I *don't* know why they don't just call it a valley!" she added quickly, forestalling his next question and making him laugh again.

"Scoot, now." She waved an airy hand. "The librarian wants to get these new books covered, stickered and on display before we leave."

Humming, Davey skipped back to his corner. Maura recognized the tune and took it up softly under her breath: "The farmer in the dell, the farmer in the dell, Heigho! the derry-oh, the farmer in the dell."

She smoothed a hand over the next book on her desk. *Techniques of the Organic Gardener.* The binding popped as she opened the cover. She inhaled the new-book smell of the pages and scanned the table of contents, noticing some of the terms Nate had used and even some she knew herself. She felt an overwhelming urge to turn the page and start reading and forget the other books stacked on her desk awaiting her attention.

Her gaze wandered to them, and Maura bit her lower lip in a spasm of retrospective guilt. Though she was obligated as librarian to purchase books that would either serve the needs of the community or that would fill a hole in the library's collection, she'd ordered this book solely for her own interest. She'd been scrupulously conscientious in every purchase after this one, but she knew the guilt came from another source. She'd bought the book to learn more of what Nate Farrell cared about so greatly.

Though she hadn't seen him since the evening a week ago when they'd shared her stew, he was constantly in her thoughts, mostly, she figured, because of the issues he'd raised. He'd brought up many a farming concept she agreed with, but more than that he'd stimulated her curiosity, bringing on a thirst for knowledge much like Davey's. She wanted to know more, even if the techniques fell outside of the purview of the Master Gardener program, to satisfy a need within her—a need, like Nate's, to do right by the land.

Over the past week, she'd found herself thinking more than a few times *I've got to remember to ask Nate about such-and-such,* or *I've got to tell him how thus-and-so happened.* Then she'd remember herself, a stab of disappointment hitting even before she recognized the consequences of inviting such an encounter. Because much as she craved the satisfaction of talking to someone who understood a vital part of her, she couldn't encourage any sort of relationship, friendly or otherwise, with Nate Farrell. Because she could tell he wanted more.

"The farmer takes a wife, the farmer takes a wife," Davey sang in his off-key but enthusiastic child-voice, "heigho! the derry-oh, the farmer takes a wife."

Maura's thoughts drifted back to the other subjects she and Nate had covered. It had been awkward talking about Wayne and the fight between him and Nate, but it had also been a relief. Over the past two years, she'd wished desperately for someone to talk to about Wayne, about her fears and the terrible emotions that his death had produced in her:

anger, helplessness and guilt. Her minister had provided comfort, told her it was perfectly normal for her to feel these things and gave her guidance on how to get past them and go on living. In this instance, however, *she* needed more. She wanted to talk to someone who knew—like Doreen. But even though her mother-in-law was dealing with her own widowhood, how could Maura say "I'm angry with your son for dying, for leaving me alone in a world where anything can happen—where the worst *has* happened"?

She would have even liked to talk to Kenny, Wayne's younger brother. But it was less an option. Kenny was still having problems with both his father's and his brother's deaths. He'd worshiped the two men. When Doreen, Kenny, Davey and Maura got together, Kenny maintained an unstated pretense of his father and brother being only temporarily missing from the group. Nothing explicit had ever been said, but it was very clear, and very sad, that Kenny had a long way to go in dealing with his own emotions.

So now ironically Maura had found understanding and solace in the unlikely person of Nate Farrell. Their sharing, however, brought back all the memories of how he'd made her feel those years ago and reinforced how alike those feelings were to ones she experienced now.

And what exactly were those feelings? she asked herself. Wariness, a little bit of fear, a lot of a perverse fascination. It all boiled down to what she'd thought the day he plowed her garden: Nate Farrell was too intense. At seventeen, she'd seen that intensity and felt its pull like a magnet—almost as much as it had repelled her. For all Wayne's rage that made him strike out at Nate so fiercely, it had paled in significance to the force behind Nate's single blow.

No, Nate Farrell didn't want more; he wanted it all. Her father had simplified Nate's objective down to *that boy's looking for a wife.* As she'd told Nate the other night, she realized how ridiculous her father's accusation had been. Because Nate hadn't been looking for a wife then; he wasn't now. What he *was* looking for, wanting, needing, even expecting, was a commitment that matched his own. In everything.

Maura recalled the conviction in Nate's voice as he'd spoken of his plans for his farm. She admired his determination even as she ached for him, almost in the same way she ached for Davey when she saw him struggle against an uncompromising world. *Stop wanting so much,* she wished to tell her son and make him understand. She often thought of the short prayer that, over the past two years, she found had helped her so greatly:

Grant me serenity to accept what cannot be changed, courage to change what should be changed, and wisdom to distinguish the one from the other.

She would be the first to admit it was easier said than done, though, for while she believed she'd learned acceptance in some things, she wondered if she would ever consistently recognize courage and wisdom, especially as she raised Davey.

Maura heard the front door open around the corner. Davey's singing trailed off as she could almost see him remembering their rule: when it was just the two of them in the library, they could speak out loud, but silence was golden when other patrons were present.

She raised her head expectantly and found herself looking into Nate Farrell's blue-gray eyes.

"'Evening, Maura," he said, accordingly library quiet, although the husky timbre of his words seemed to ring in the stillness.

"Hello, Nate." A billow of chagrin mixed with pleasure inflated her chest. It crossed her mind to try to hide the subject of the book in front of her, but she was strangely happy at his unanticipated appearance and she found herself glad for this opportunity to show it to him. "Look what came in just today." She lifted the open book in both hands so he could read the cover.

His brows rose as he met her eyes over the top of the book. His lower lip jutted briefly before doing its part to contribute to his slow smile. She could tell he was pleased. For the moment, Maura ignored her circumspection about Nate and his wants and needs and gave in to the urge to talk to him about her own pursuits.

"I've been thinking about the things you're doing to preserve the soil, how you're going to go to completely organic farming," she explained excitedly. "I found this book in a catalog my first day here." Lowering the book to the desk, she ran her finger down the page. "Look, there're chapters on balanced fertility, the oxygen-ethylene cycle, biological and cultural pest control, achieving biodiversity...."

She paused on the last subject. Nate sat on the edge of her desk, twisting his neck to read, too. His breath ruffled her hair ever so softly—as softly as his touch had been on her cheek, though she had the feeling, then and now, that the purpose behind it had been unyielding.

"Do you know what biodiversification is, Maura?" he asked.

She looked up and found his face close to hers. As always, his intensity unnerved her, as he seemed to delve into her soul through her eyes. She recognized, after spending time in his company, the trait that contributed to that intensity: Nate was a keenly observant man. He had to be, of course, to be able to examine his crops day in and day out and spot small but often critical differences. Maura saw now that very little escaped his notice. He would never be one to leave any matter, even a years-old one, unsettled—as Wayne had.

But if Wayne had had a significant fault, it was his tendency to deal with life only on the surface, without recognizing the many undercurrents of emotions and motivations that could influence a person.

Maura let her gaze drop, as much to escape her thoughts as to avoid Nate's scrutiny. She focused on the page before her. "I'm not sure. Do you know what biodiversity is?"

"It's a process really. In nature there's a balance that's gotten out of whack over years and years of people doing unnatural things to and with the land. Working towards biodiversification means trying to restore the natural balance in things."

"How, though?"

Nate grasped his forearm as it rested on his thigh, clearly defined beneath the denim. "Well, in farming, for example, I'm untiling parts of my land—taking out the drainage tiles—and turning some of the low-lying areas, which I had to double plant more often than not when they flooded in the spring, back to marsh and wetlands. It'll take some years, but fish and wildlife should start returning to these areas, and their benefits will start accumulating. The birds that eat harmful insects will return. The aquifer—the water table—gets cleaner as the marsh filters the chemicals that ran through it before. And as the groundwater and the soil's minerals slowly become more balanced, I can grow uncontaminated crops and my livestock eats healthier." He spread his hands. "It's a total commitment and it takes time. A lot of time. But in the end, everything works together again."

"And it drastically changes the face of farming in Iowa," she said as the information sank in. Restoring nature's balance—no, it really wasn't a commitment one could "sort of" make. Isn't that what she'd just been thinking about Nate? All or nothing in a way that seemed unnegotiable. But one *couldn't* undertake such a project in half measures.

Everything works together, but only if everything is pledged to that end.

Maura noticed a glaze of withdrawal had begun to film Nate's eyes as she sat mulling over his words. She knew he found it difficult to talk about his work—about anything really, as most private people did.

She gave him a supportive smile. "I wanted to tell you, Nate, how much I enjoyed our supper together. I never guessed you could be so... I mean, you really sparked my interest by the way you..."

Maura let her voice trail off as she realized she'd been about to tell the reserved and untalkative Nate Farrell that she found him... *Eloquent* was still the only word that defined his thoughtful, unassuming explanation of his plans. *Eloquent*—though certainly he struggled in expressing himself. But he'd done so in his own words, and each word had counted. Perhaps *eloquent* could be defined as being able to speak from the heart, Maura thought, though she doubted the dictionary at her elbow would concur.

"You made me realize," she went on, "how little I know about both horticulture and agriculture. I guess I was feeling kind of cocky about my Master Gardener training, but it just touched the tip of the iceberg, didn't it? I keep wondering, really, what insights I'll be able to bring to gardeners in town."

The warmth returned to Nate's eyes at her comments. "You know enough to help people learn some new things and to troubleshoot the kinds of problems they'll have. You're not aiming to start a revolution, Maura," he said with a straight face, though she noticed the quirk of his lips. "That's my job."

"Afraid of the competition?" she bantered as a strange but pleasurable quiver shot through her. When he smiled or laughed or teased, it was always quietly, making it more special. And more memorable.

She caught a movement in the corner of her vision. Davey stood ten feet away, half-hidden by a shelf of books as he observed the two of them. Absently he picked at the ragged corner of a book cover, his solemn little face clearly depicting his reluctance to interrupt their adult conversation. She wondered how long he'd been standing there.

Maura smiled her encouragement even as it occurred to her how thoroughly absorbed she could become in Nate Farrell.

Still Davey looked uncertain as his gaze flickered to Nate, who sat with his back to the boy. Then Nate stood, turning toward the object of her attention, and spied Davey.

"Hey, pardner," Nate said, and Davey broke into a grin as she realized the reason for her·son's hesitancy: he'd been unsure of Nate, of whether the connection that had taken root a week ago had survived the ensuing separation.

Nate extended a hand, palm down, toward the boy. Davey shuffled forward and, to Maura's amazement, the boy ducked his head to fit its crown into the cup of that large open hand. She saw Nate's fingers tighten in the gold hair, giving Davey's head a little shake. Davey's response was subtle but profound: a brief and blissful closing of his eyes.

Bleakness swept over her.

It was a manly caress—gruff, nonchalant—yet it spoke volumes to her. Lately Davey had begun avoiding such touches from her. She almost had to sneak them in when he was tired or in a tickling match. It wasn't that she didn't understand—he was at the age where he equated caresses with comfort and comfort with babying. But she realized now that, with his seeking Nate's touch, it was far more complex. She recalled the long, dark nights after Wayne's death, in which she'd held her son's sleeping body close to her and found that the only way she could endure the pain was to concentrate on the gentle in-out-in-out of his breathing. And after he'd had his operation and begun wearing his glasses, she'd spent many a day never more than an arm's length from him, finding it unimaginable to think he might reach out for her and not find her there.

Now it was almost as if Davey believed, as much as a five-year-old could reason, that the time and need for such reassurances between them was over and that to satisfy them any longer was self-indulgent. *She* needed those caresses, not him.

Yet Nate's touch and attention were something different. In seeking out Nate, Davey was taking a step toward the recovery she'd long prayed he'd make. Her little boy was learning to trust again, after having had the most basic of childhood securities jerked out from under him. He was learning to believe in the future again—yet it was coming about through Nate.

Maura glanced up at Nate and she knew some of her thoughts showed on her face. Giving the boy's head a final pat, he dropped his hand. A blush of shame crept up her neck.

How could she act so pettily! She should be glad Davey was taking to Nate so well. She was just being overprotective, as she'd been telling herself for weeks. Even Davey could tell.

"Closing time," she told her son with a forgiving smile. "Are all the books put away and chairs straight?"

"Uh-huh," Davey assured her with a nod. Already he knew the routine.

"Good." Maura straightened her desk as she did every evening, putting away her date stamps and shelf-list cards. She hesitated a moment when she picked up the gardening book, then set it on top of the others she would have to finish processing tomorrow.

"Maura," Nate said.

"Yes?" she said pleasantly, looking up at him, Davey still at his side.

His mouth tightened. "I came in tonight to tell you that Little League starts in a few days. I thought maybe you'd like to sign Davey up."

Her son's eyes grew round as quarters. "Little League?" he breathed.

"Baseball." Nate grasped an imaginary bat and did a slow swing, ending up with clasped hands next to his left shoulder in follow-through. He cracked a smile at Davey before catching Maura's eye out of the corner of his own.

She saw his smile die at her dismayed expression. Of course Nate had only good intentions, but he should have broached the subject to her alone! Now Davey would be disappointed, no doubt about it from the way he was looking at her, much the same as he had when Nate suggested going to Ernie's.

"Honey, could you wait for me outside on the bench? I want to talk to Nate for a minute."

Some of the light went out of her son's eyes at her gentle but neutral tone. "Okay, Mama." He gave Nate a quick smile—a goodbye and good luck all at once. Then he turned to Maura, freckled face solemn and contemplative.

"Daddy liked baseball, didn't he, Mama?" he said. "I 'member him watching it on TV. And he played catch with me. Didn't he?"

"Y-yes," Maura stammered, and swallowed. "Your dad loved baseball."

Davey nodded. "I remember."

With that, her son left. She heard the door shut behind him with a soft *thunk*.

Drawing in a shuddering breath, Maura covered her face with her hands, uncertain whether to cry or sing. She often wondered what Davey remembered of Wayne. On occasion, she'd bring up some routine or entertainment the three of them had shared, only to have Davey stare at her in bewilderment. That look never failed to cut into her, making her feel a discouraging inadequacy.

"He was only three," she defended them both.

"Maura—"

She heard Nate take a step. Then she felt the warmth of his palm on the crown of her own head in a caress much like that which he'd bestowed on Davey. And, tender and potent, the warmth of his hand produced in her a reaction she guessed was similar to her son's: a slow flow of understanding and acceptance. *It's okay to feel this way.* It was the same response she'd had when Nate had touched her as they stood in his yard. Like before, she simultaneously yearned

toward it and shied away from it in a confusing tug-of-war
with her deepest impulses. The only conclusion she could
come to was that she couldn't allow him to continue touching her. Once already she'd nearly come to tears in front of
him, had almost lost control.

Calmly Maura lifted her head, leaning back and out of
range of his reach. "I'm afraid it won't work out to put
Davey in Little League," she said. "First of all, he's too
young. Don't the boys have to be in school, even the Tee-
Ballers? And the practices are mostly before supper. I work
until six and, with the ball diamond clear on the other side
of town, it's too far for Davey to walk there and back by
himself. He doesn't have a glove," she declared, a little angry that she should have to admit that costs were a concern,
even for a boy's baseball glove. "And you shouldn't have
mentioned it in front of Davey, Nate. He's going to be disappointed."

At her words, she saw Nate's jaw work, the Farrell chin
stiffen. "I didn't intend to, but—*durn.*" He shifted onto one
leg in a determined pose. "I thought Davey could ride back
and forth to practice with me. And most of the older kids
who've moved up to the adult size have their used Little
League gloves stashed away somewhere. I could probably
get Davey one for under ten bucks."

She was surprised. He'd obviously thought about this.
"What about his age?" she asked.

"Yeah, well." Nate ran his hand through his hair in a
gesture Maura had already learned was a sure sign of his
uneasiness. He glanced almost nervously at the door. "I got
the age requirement waived."

She blinked. "How?"

"Because I'll be coaching the Tee-Ballers."

He jammed his fingers into the front pockets of his jeans
and looked at her squarely. "Harv Middleton was set to do
it, but he's got an opportunity to work some overtime at the
plant, and he and his wife've got that new baby—" He cut
himself off, looking strangely disgusted with his explana-

tion. "They needed a coach," he said tersely. "And I thought it'd be good for Davey. Maybe help you out."

A bittersweet blend of respect and regret mingled in her breast. Yes, he'd obviously been thinking—about Davey, about helping her. But she wasn't sure she wanted help, especially Nate's. Davey was becoming attached to him. Watching them together, she realized there was a need in Davey that was going unmet, but *she* wanted the chance to fill that need! And she couldn't let Nate become a part of the boy's life, because she couldn't let him become a part of *her* life.

Was that it? Was he thinking he might get to her through Davey? she thought a little indignantly.

Could he?

She looked at him, stance fixed and steadfast in the wake of her objections. Whatever his reasons, Nate had put himself on the line here, and she knew it hadn't been easy for him to do so.

"What about the talk around town about your farming, Nate?" she asked. "I'd hate to see you put yourself in a position to draw more fire."

"I can take care of myself, Maura." At that moment, he looked as clearly indomitable as his assertion.

"Yes, you can," she murmured. "But can Davey? What if he isn't ready to start playing baseball? I mean, won't he be behind the others in development? At that age, even a few months makes a difference."

"Is that what's worrying you? That it'll do Davey more harm than good if he can't keep up with the other boys?"

"I'm worried because...he takes so much to heart." She closed her eyes, then opened them with a shake of her head when the images etched on her lids wouldn't go away. "Davey never mourned his father very much, Nate. For a long time I thought he simply didn't realize what had happened. Then about eight months after Wayne's death, we started treatment for his lazy eye, weakened because of his crossed eye. The ophthalmologist put a patch on the good one and...Davey fought it, so fiercely. He couldn't see—he was plunged into a world of shadows. I understood his frustration, that partly he was venting some of his anger about Wayne. Maybe even some anger at me for letting something like that happen. Then after the lazy eye regained most of its sight, he had his operation, and I thought that would be it. But he still needed glasses, they said. And after the way he dealt with the patch...I didn't know how much more either of us could take. He took to the glasses, though, almost too much. The ophthalmologist says it's the best thing Davey could do, but..."

"Are you afraid Davey will find out his eyesight is still not quite normal if he's learning some intensive eye-hand co-ordination?"

"No. The doctor said his eyes are doing beautifully. It's not that. It's just that I can't help feeling he uses his glasses for security. For distance. And I don't know how to handle a child who...who fights his battles within his own head, where I can't help him."

His gaze dropped, and Nate frowned thoughtfully. "I told you before, I'm no expert," he said slowly, "but I think it'd be pretty hard to raise a child who's a lot like you. Especially when he shows inclinations you might not be too fond of in yourself."

He wore the expression of a man delivering unwelcome news, but Maura was merely surprised. "Davey's like me?"

"I think he is. For instance, you can tell when things are really bothering you and Davey."

"You can?"

"Sure. You both get a worry line right here." He sketched a vertical stroke between his brows with his thumbnail. "I suppose it isn't obvious, with his glasses on most of the time. But he looks just like you when he gets it."

Her hand rose almost of its own accord, and she found the ridge of flesh right where Nate said it was. *Add "worrywart" to "overprotective" and "petty."* She could see his point. "I'd been thinking lately that I've become quite a brooder over the last few years," she said ruefully.

His gaze gentled in understanding. "It's natural, given what you've both gone through."

Again Nate Farrell was providing comfort, understanding and a perception she hadn't grasped herself. "I guess I'd always seen traces of Wayne, more than myself, in Davey," she explained lamely.

"Oh, he's your son, all right, in case you ever had a doubt." He paused, aimed his gaze at the door again, then he brought those blue-gray eyes around to focus on her. "But he's also Wayne's, and Wayne was a natural at baseball. It wouldn't surprise me if Davey's inherited some of that talent, enough to give him a little bit of a head start on some of the kids. Finding out he can do something he's not half-bad at might help him gain some confidence."

He was right, of course. Getting Davey into Little League was a perfect way to bring the boy out of his shell. She'd been pleased with his interest in books and had been encouraging him to help her in the garden, mostly because she found such satisfaction working there. She hoped he might derive a similar pleasure, but just because poking around in the dirt helped her didn't mean it would help Davey. Even if it did, perhaps it simply wasn't what he needed most right now.

Baseball. How fitting that this sport would stir Davey's memory of Wayne. But she and Davey, and now Nate, were making new memories every day. Without Wayne.

Would playing baseball bring Davey closer to his father's memory—or closer to Nate? Because though today it was baseball, tomorrow it'd be football and first shaves, then girls and cars, and after that....

Her throat swelled with nostalgia—and something else. It wasn't that she wanted yesterday back or to keep tomorrow at bay. She simply wanted to hold on to the familiar present. To take things, as she had for two years, one day at a time.

But this man, in his own irrepressible way, was taking her into the uncharted future. In him dwelt a unique blend of dreamer and doer. For Nate, Maura realized, the future held a great promise.

Once again she felt that sense of being pulled by a magnet, out of control of her own destiny—and Davey's.

Truly I want only what's best for Davey.

"I tell you what," she finally said. "I'll check with Doreen to see if she can pick Davey up after practice if you'll come by here to take him there. Maybe Kenny, Wayne's brother, can pitch in and help you out, though he's on the road most of the time. And I'd appreciate it if you'd ask around about a glove for Davey. Let me know the other fees involved, too. Will he need a uniform?"

"Not for this age group. We've got a sponsor who provides stenciled T-shirts and caps, and the boys wear them with their jeans and sneakers. The safety helmets are provided by the program."

"Fine."

A slight awkwardness hung between them, the lingering effects of discord, although it had diminished as they talked.

"Thank you, Nate," Maura said. "For thinking of Davey and for listening to me. Again. You know, I can't really talk to Doreen about Davey."

"Well, you can talk to me anytime, Maura," he answered, and obviously meant it. Once more she felt at war with her reactions to Nate Farrell. He inspired such conflicting feelings—a sense of sanctuary while still a definite threat. A long-awaited answer that only raised a million more questions.

She indicated the door. "I guess you'd better go tell what I can imagine is one impatiently squirming boy that he's been recruited for Little League. I'll be out in a minute."

Nate smiled. "I'll keep an eye on him at practices, Maura. And I wouldn't worry about him catching on—most of the kids that age flail around. It's all for fun."

Maura had to smile back despite her qualms. "You're the coach."

He gave her a nod and left.

Reaching into her purse, Maura found her checkbook. She hesitated as her gaze lit on her penciled balance. Things really weren't that tight. Her finances were actually in good shape, but only because she'd been careful about sticking to her budget. Because she'd been a worrywart.

Her gaze fell to the book on top of the stack on her desk. *Techniques of the Organic Gardener.* She reached out, hesitated, then picked up the book, tucking it under her arm as she stood, giving her library a last visual going-over.

"Okay, now we can go home," she proclaimed to the empty room.

Nate's knock sounded tinnily on Maura's screen door. Into June now, the twilight lingered longer, making the after-supper hours some of the best of the day. He'd almost bet Maura would be working in her garden, but no—here she came through the house to the front door.

"Nate?" she said rather breathlessly as she pushed a lock of hair out of her eyes and opened the door. He recognized her gardening attire. She was dressed in a pair of jeans and an oversize work shirt whose tails hung to midthigh.

"'Evening, Maura. Giving those tomato plants a piece of your mind, were you?" he asked.

"I, uh, I guess," she said, unresponsive to his quip. In fact, she seemed distracted. "I was out back and came in just this minute."

Obviously she'd been deep in one of her daydreams. "I don't mean to keep you, but I wanted to drop this off for Davey." He held up a small leather baseball glove. "I finally went by Bobby Donaldson's to get it after waiting a week and a half for him to remember to bring it to practice."

"Oh. Sure." Looking as if she were reluctantly accepting a telegram that contained bad news, Maura took the glove from Nate. He wasn't surprised by the ensuing aggravation that rose in him. No, she wasn't distracted, he concluded. He hated it when she got that apprehensive look on her face, as if he meant her harm, like some bully on a playground who picked on the younger kids just for the fun of it.

Would he ever get past her fear?

"Fine," he said shortly, seeking that precious distance. "Well, I'll be on my way."

"What do I owe you?"

It made him feel chintzy to nickel and dime her, but he'd learned on two previous occasions that Maura was sensitive about paying her and Davey's way. "I gave Lucy Donaldson six bucks even though she said she was only too glad to clear a little of the junk out of Bobby's closet."

Maura nodded. "Six dollars it is." Again she hesitated, held him at bay, then her expression softened. "Why don't you come in while I find my billfold?"

Shucking off his hat and holding it in one hand while he smoothed his hair down with the other, Nate stepped into the narrow foyer and followed Maura down the hall. He got a glimpse of a living room and a bedroom along the way to the back of the house. Although this was the first time he'd set foot in this house, he would bet it hadn't looked like this when Hank Peterson lived here. His gaze roamed around the kitchen, with its bright curtains that matched the table-cloth, the ceramic canisters shaped like mushrooms arranged in graduating sizes on the counter, the other dashes and splashes of color and gladness that made him think he was almost looking at Maura herself.

"This is real pretty," he said, knowing his own home didn't make the same statement about himself. Of course, he had three-hundred-plus acres that were making more of a statement than he would have liked.

Maura looked startled by his announcement, then pleased in that way he liked: the soft glow spreading across her cheeks, a shy lowering of lashes.

Nate's fingers spasmodically crushed the springy mesh of his cap. Lord, maybe she should be afraid.

"I've been getting things done in bits and pieces as I have time," she said. "I just finished Davey's room last week."

"Is that the one we passed? With the cowboys on the wall?"

"Of course. Want to see it?"

"Cowboys are a personal favorite of mine," he drawled.

She dimpled at his teasing, and he was glad she seemed more at ease now, excited to be showing off her handiwork. Again she led the way, and Nate stepped into the tiny bedroom with her. "I found a sheet set in a cowboy theme on sale," she explained, gesturing. "So I bought an extra set and used the fitted one for curtains. The flat I soaked in a mixture of water and liquid starch and pasted it to this wall to dry, see? Quick and inexpensive. I got it out of a magazine."

"I see." Nate looked around the cheery room any boy would have died for. "Does Davey like it?" he asked, knowing the answer but wanting to see the incandescent pride come to Maura's eyes.

"Davey's thrilled with it."

Forced physically closer by the confines of the small room, they shared an intimate glance, one in which Nate was allowed to look into her eyes, momentarily absent of their usual guard, and he realized he'd found another key to Maura Foster.

"Show me what else you've done," he murmured.

"There's not much," Maura demurred, but gave him the full two-dollar tour anyway.

Yes, Nate thought as he listened to her, watched her animated features, *here's another key.* He was guessing, but it came to him that she found it novel to keep a home for which she was financially responsible. Not that he was so backward he thought the notion of a woman supporting herself uncommon. It was Maura who found the experience unique and obviously satisfying, for it meant something entirely different to her. Likely she'd never expected to be in the position of being the sole breadwinner, and she was proud to know she could rise to the challenge.

But then, she hadn't had much choice.

She showed him the homey living room with its practical neutral tones and plants everywhere, the postage-stamp-sized bath. Even her bedroom, though Nate found it hard to concentrate as she related how she'd made the ruffle and pillow shams for her bed out of a flowered-print fabric. On her dresser, he saw an array of picture frames—photos of her and Davey. And Davey and Wayne. Although when he looked closer, Nate saw that it was actually Kenny Foster, Wayne's brother, with Doreen, too. Nowhere, at least not in Maura's bedroom, was there a picture of Wayne.

They finished up the tour in the kitchen again. Maura spied the glove on the table. "Here I am rattling on, and you came in for your money," she said, reaching for her purse. "How much did you say it was?"

"Six dollars," Nate answered, and when she gave him the money, he acknowledged her efforts with a smile as he fit the bills into his wallet. "He's doing real well so far, you know. At practice."

"I'm... glad," she said, sounding as though she was anything but.

"Really." Nate felt compelled to reassure her. "He's throwing better than kids two years older. His catching and batting skills are about par, though. He's getting some attention with that arm," he said proudly. He knew Maura had had misgivings about Davey's abilities. "Susie Henderson's taken quite a shine to him, even though she's got nearly as good accuracy."

"A girl?"

"Sure. They let girls play now. Makes coaching a little more complicated, though. Put a little girl with big hazel eyes and long red pigtails in the equation, and pretty soon you got a bunch of show-offs. Attention spans go to the dogs. But like I said, Davey's holding his own."

With undue concentration, Maura straightened the cloth on the table between them. "It's nice he's making friends. He's very excited about playing. It's all he can talk about, in fact."

Nate smiled, pleased to know he'd brought that kind of enthusiasm to the normally subdued boy. "Where is Davey?" he asked.

For whatever reason, the wariness came back to her face. "He's outside." She stood next to the sink, and her slight movement sideways made it look as if she were blocking his view out the window behind her.

"Is he helping you with the garden?"

"Not this evening. He's... We're digging a hole," she said somewhat defiantly.

"A hole? You mean you're planting a tree or something?"

"No." She glanced at his face, and a glimmer of dry amusement appeared on hers at his expression. "I asked him what *he* wanted to do around the place, you know, to make it his, too. First he said he wouldn't mind building a doghouse, but I got the impression he'd want to put a dog in it if we did that. Then he said a tree house would be nice, but the fork in that walnut tree is a good twelve feet off the ground, and I told him I thought we should wait till he was a little older before we built a tree house. So then he suggested digging a hole."

"A hole." He couldn't stifle the chuckle that rose to his lips.

"I know. I think he's looking for more Indian-head nickels or buried treasure."

When he continued to shake his head and laugh, she dismissed him with a flip of her hand, though a wry smile touched her own lips. "Come on, Nate. Didn't you ever want to dig a hole when you were a little boy?"

"Sure I did." He crossed his arms and leaned back against the refrigerator. "Once Drew and I—shoot, I guess we were about six or so—we thought we'd find out how far it was to

China. I got this big old serving spoon from my mom's kitchen, and Drew got a ladle and a mixing bowl—because we were going to need a place for all the dirt—from his. We gouged half a dozen divots in my yard before we discovered the ground around the flower beds was a lot easier to dig than turf. Oh, and that a little water made the process a whole lot more fun.''

"I imagine your mother had something to say about that."

"Oh, yeah." He sighed and studied the tops of his boots. "Actually she didn't say much, but she sure took it out of my hide. Drew's, too. I remember us coming out of the barn, rubbing our backsides when she was through with the both of us, and Drew turned to me and said, 'Next time let's get into trouble at my house. My mom don't pack the wallop yours does.' "

Maura laughed, a throaty sound that was so like her—tranquil and lighthearted at the same time. "Well, this hole has been fully approved and sanctioned by me."

"If I were Davey, I'd still get it in writing."

The intimacy of the tiny kitchen, of the entire house, in fact, made their conversation seem more personal. More inescapably private. He wondered if Maura felt it, too. Nate knew he couldn't have lived in such close quarters himself, but right now he liked the sense of familiarity the small rooms produced between them. And it seemed to him that when he got closer to her, both physically and emotionally, he got past her fear, or at least stirred something else in her that momentarily diminished her caution.

"Need any help?" he volunteered, wanting to prolong that effect. "I mean, you can call my mother if you're wondering about my hole-digging qualifications."

Her laughter died, and Maura half turned, glancing out the window behind her. The wariness came back in force. "Thanks, Nate, but—" she faced him with a mutinous set to her mouth "—but this is our project. Davey's and mine."

Nate studied her, arms still crossed on his chest, and tried to see past that defiance while not revealing his own churning thoughts. Then he realized what was going on. Yes, Maura was proud of her independence and her ability to provide for Davey and herself. Like a mother bear with a cub, she was fiercely protective of that ability—and obviously struggling to retain it.

It made sense—her questions about his own ability to communicate with Davey right off the bat, her reluctance to encourage that connection.

He was a threat.

Nate couldn't help feeling disappointed by her resistance. He'd been thinking only to help her and, he admitted, to enjoy Davey's company. He genuinely liked the little boy, and he'd found something within him fulfilled by spending time with Davey. In a way, he thought of the changes in his farming, going to more healthy and environmentally safe ways of growing, as being for Davey's sake. For the sake of children everywhere. Seeing Davey do some growing of his own made the guff Nate took for his farming worthwhile.

So now he knew the source of her fear—or at least part of it, for he suspected there was more to the matter. But sure as the sun, he knew what he was up against. Every minute he spent with Davey counted against him as far as Maura was concerned. There was no help for it now, though. He was committed to coaching Davey's team. And durn it, he wanted to! Where was the harm in it? After all, it wasn't as if he could steal Davey's love from Maura.

Unless it wasn't Davey's love for her she was worried about.

His teeth sank into his upper lip as he continued to study her. For a moment longer she stared back, and he realized he found her gentle defiance incredibly attractive, rousing the best and the worst of his instincts. And it made him do something a little bit wicked.

"Could I trouble you for a drink of water?" he asked even as he took the two steps in her tiny kitchen to bring him next to the sink. And closer to her, he told himself, just to see what she'd do.

She reacted as he'd guessed she would. More of that delectable defiance, a little bit of that exasperating fear. She moved away to reach into one of the cupboards. He ignored the glass she held out and turned on the faucet, letting the water run through his fingers as it grew cooler. Nate pointedly avoided looking out to the backyard where Davey was, and he saw out of the corner of his eye that neither was Maura's attention aimed out the window. Instead, she watched the cascade of water into his palm. Watched as he lifted his cupped hand to his lips and drank. And stared—as she had the day he tilled her garden—when he wiped his mouth with the edge of his index finger.

Rubbing his wet hand down the leg of his jeans, he finally turned toward her. Her gaze remained fixed on his mouth as if mesmerized, and Nate found himself equally mesmerized. It made him take a chance. Reaching out, he slid his hand under her chin and, with a slowness that belied the rage of fire that sprang up in him of a sudden, he touched his lips to hers.

God, could there be anything softer? Soft and sweet, inviting as a spring day. Nate nestled his mouth more securely into that softness as he rested his other hand on her waist. He choked back a groan at the feel of that nipped-in curve hidden beneath her voluminous shirt. He liked the dresses she wore better than these clothes, dresses like flowers in both color and nature, the way she bloomed in them. The way they accented her womanly shape, the slight but fascinating fullness of breast and hip that, in his perception, was never lost by a woman who'd borne a child.

Wayne Foster's child.

At that thought, Nate pulled Maura closer, his reaction as instinctive as Maura's had been for Davey a few minutes before. Not protective. Territorial.

At the increase in contact and pressure, Maura tensed. Nate eased his hold on her slightly. *Don't be afraid* was the message he hoped to convey, but he felt her mouth tremble under his and he knew he couldn't continue such torment of her. Whatever the reason he frightened her, it was real. And once more Nate found himself backing off where Maura Foster was concerned. For now.

He lifted his head and stepped back, letting her go. Her eyes downcast, she put out a steadying hand, gripping the edge of the sink, her agitation palpable.

"I guess I'll be going," he said after a moment. "You and Davey can certainly handle digging a hole yourselves." He gave her what he hoped was a sympathetic smile. She certainly had a trial before her, more than just raising Davey and providing for him. And Nate knew he had a trial before him, for he walked a thin line not between mother and child, but between past and future. He wasn't looking to take Wayne's place in Davey's heart, if that's what Maura feared, but he would take Wayne's place in her heart, if it were the only way.

The decision didn't come easily to him. He felt a stab of guilt knowing he would be challenging her and her most sacred memories. But he was here; he was now. This was his biggest advantage.

Nate picked up his cap, lying on the counter, and slapped it against his thigh. "Tell Davey I'll see him at practice tomorrow."

"Okay," Maura agreed, though Nate had doubts she really would mention his visit to the boy.

He gave a last glance around the kitchen, at the evidence of her hard work. Maura was a lot like his sister, Callie, he decided. Like his mother, too. All three were women who had inherited the survival instincts of their pioneering ancestors. Like a lone pine he'd once seen growing out of the crest of a limestone bluff, theirs was an unpretentious perseverance, one of stark beauty. They simply endured and went on. And whatever Maura's fears for herself and Davey, she would endure.

"You've done a nice job with this house," he said, giving her the credit she deserved—and perhaps did not receive enough of.

"Thank you. I've still got lots I want to do." Her message was clear, as it had been that evening at his house.

His was equally clear. "You'll do it, even if it takes longer than you'd like."

He couldn't find it in himself to regret kissing her, for even if her reaction had been less than enthusiastic, he felt he'd gotten past some barrier she'd put up, for just a moment. Long enough for her to register it, long enough for it to make her think. And wonder. As for himself, he knew now that this time he would not relinquish his chance with Maura for any reason.

Nate left her in the kitchen and let himself out the front door. Even while inhaling heartily of the sweet outdoors, he realized that, for the first time in memory, he didn't experience that sense of emancipation he always felt in escaping the confines of a building. And it had been Maura's little two-by-four cottage to boot. It didn't take a leap in logic for Nate to conclude that he could get used to closeness if it meant being close to Maura.

Maybe he was getting smarter after all.

Chapter Five

Nate had taught Davey how to whistle.

Maura paused in drafting the outline of her talk for the Soldier Creek Garden Club and gazed out the library window as she pictured her son. He went about with his lips in a constant pucker, emitting breathy toots that over days were becoming more substantial. He'd even attempted a tune or two: a barely recognizable "Mary Had a Little Lamb" or "Three Blind Mice" were constant accompaniments to the normal sounds around their house these days. Whenever the whistling died out, Maura could count on looking up to find Davey concentrating on snapping his fingers, a skill that still eluded him. However, his greatest aspiration, he'd informed her, was to learn how to whistle through his teeth, as Nate did with eardrum-piercing facility when rounding the team up for practice.

That's where Davey was now, at practice, an after-supper one on her late-closing night. She had to admit she missed him, though his absence allowed her to get a lot of work done. It was always quiet on Thursday evenings and, with

Davey gone, she found she could concentrate on more thought-intensive projects like researching topics for her Master Gardener speeches. They were becoming quite popular. After her first talk at the Garden Club, she'd been asked to speak to the Good Morning Circle and the Ladies' Aid, with requests for return engagements.

And the talks had gone wonderfully. Nate had been right: she had something new to teach these women. Many had been gardening for years, like her, but hadn't kept up with some of the new techniques and options that were available to them. They gardened much as their mothers had and, as Nate had observed, weren't apt to explore other ways of tending their gardens simply because there had never been a reason to change. Not when their gardens were producing as much as they always had.

Maura knew her task was twofold: showing people how they *could* get better yields from their gardens and teaching them how to do it cost-effectively through determining the best course of action, especially in pest management. They already knew how to prevent worms from attacking their tomatoes by pushing a large juice can into the dirt around the plant. It was going to take some convincing, however, to keep them from immediately marching down to the lumberyard for a fungicide when the spots on their zucchini leaves might be perfectly harmless if unsightly.

Again Maura thought of Nate and his efforts. In fact, she found herself using him as an illustration of certain techniques, though it wasn't strictly proper for her to digress from the Master Gardener program into organic farming. At first the ladies had reacted with thin-lipped silence to the mention of Nate's methods. Maura realized that, as with the older farmers who were voicing criticism of Nate, these ladies felt threatened. They were being asked to change; their ways were being challenged, and it was a hard for them to contemplate that, in addition to perhaps not doing things the best way, they might possibly be doing harm.

Yet by using nonconfrontational persuasion, Maura managed to get past these obstacles. By the second meeting, she found herself regularly answering questions about helping the environment. She hoped she wasn't doing Nate more harm than good by making him the main topic at every supper table in Soldier Creek, but she sensed quite strongly that though the questions were sometimes skeptical or idly curious, by and large these women wanted to know for the good of their families, which were their responsibility.

It helped that most of what Nate was doing made sense on a fundamental level. And Maura's listeners, good Iowa women, were rich in common sense. Even if their husbands had yet to do so, they realized that much had been "undone" to the environment over the years. They wanted to repair the damage—if Maura would show them how.

And each time she outlined Nate's endeavor, his aims and hers became a little more tightly enmeshed. And her heart became a little closer to him.

The crash of the front door against its hinges brought Maura's head around in alarm. She recognized little Susie Henderson, who stood panting, her hand holding the door open apparently to aid in what she clearly anticipated would be an equally turbulent exit. Her eyes were wide with apprehension, and Maura recognized the look at once. Susie had bad news.

The hair on the back of Maura's neck rose. Remembered sensations assaulted her: first a muffled explosion, the disorienting shaking of the ground, then mountainous clouds of blue-black smoke, followed by an acrid, penetrating smell carried on the wind in heated gusts.

What was that? The co-op! Oh, my God...

"Mrs. Foster!"

Maura realized Susie had called her name more than once. "Where's Davey?" she asked urgently.

"Coach sent me. He took Dave to your house. I think his forehead's cut, not too bad, but...his glasses got smashed."

"Did he—" Maura swallowed, her throat clogged with inexpressible fears, her heart bursting—or breaking—within her. *Not his eyes. Please, not his eyes.* A thundercloud of self-recriminations gathered in her chest, and only her imminent concern for Davey's condition kept it from loosing itself. "Did a ball hit him?"

"No," Susie assured her. "It was a fight."

Grabbing her purse, Maura was out of her chair before Susie had finished her sentence. She locked the library behind her and, opening her car door, hustled the little girl across the front seat. Maura got in after her as Susie offered snatches of explanations: "Tommy Lee...calling names...Four Eyes...Dave ignored him but then...he called Coach crazy...Crazy Nate...I *hate* that Tommy Lee!"

With effort, Maura managed not to speed during the half mile home, telling herself that Davey was fine, Nate would have taken him to the doctor if the child had been seriously injured.

But oh, her little boy! His precious glasses that kept the world contained for him—they could be patched back together, replaced if necessary, but not her son's barely mended spirit.

"Quickly, Susie, tell me what happened."

From what Susie told her, Tommy had waited until Nate was otherwise occupied and started picking on Davey, calling him names. Davey had ignored him, which only made Tommy madder. When Davey turned his back on the older boy, tried to walk away from a confrontation, Tommy had pushed him from behind. Davey had a ball in his glove, Susie said, and Maura guessed that it'd kept him from being able to break his fall. He'd hit the ground face first, driving the upper edge of his frames into his forehead.

Even then, Susie explained, Davey held his temper as she rushed to his side. This apparently infuriated Tommy, who, Maura had by now surmised, was taken with the little girl. That's when Tommy had delivered the last of his taunts and, according to Susie, the worst as far as Davey was concerned: the coach, whom Davey obviously adored, was nothing more than Crazy Nate. Maura took it that this set Davey into a frenzy. She had a brief vision of Wayne's face as he charged Nate like a raging bull.

Nate had intervened shortly thereafter, Susie said, after making an apparently spectacular vault over the outfield fence where he'd been fetching a stray ball. He had to pull Davey off the older boy, who escaped with a split lip.

Maura turned the car into her driveway, parked and ran to the house, leaving Susie to follow as best she could. Inside, she found a deserted living room. Hearing voices, she tracked them to the open door of Davey's bedroom.

Nate squatted in front of Davey, who sat on the edge of his bed facing away from her. Awkwardly Nate was daubing antiseptic on Davey's face with a cotton ball that looked as insubstantial as a snowflake between his large fingers. He kept up a steady stream of patter about Davey's being such a tough soldier and he'd bet the boy wouldn't even have a scar, but if he did it would be a fine-looking one, like a pirate's, and very enviable if Nate knew anything about kids these days. Not a sound came from her son as he braced one hand on the bedspread against the antiseptic's sting, followed by the pressure of a bandage being applied. Clasped in that hand was one half of his glasses. The other half lay near his thigh. The plastic safety lens was cracked down the middle, clearly unsalvageable.

Maura's hand went to her lips to stifle a moan as her heart went out to her son.

Nate looked up and caught her expression. He left Davey's side and strode over to her. His hands closed over her upper arms as he obstructed her sight of Davey, or perhaps Davey's sight of her.

"He's all right!" he whispered roughly, his face ravaged with the prospect of his own culpability in this incident. "He's got a cut over his brow, nothing serious, but that's all!"

She looked up into his eyes and registered his instruction that she get a grip on herself. Taking a deep breath and letting it out from her diaphragm, Maura did feel better, calmer. It helped to have Nate's invincible presence so close, shoring her up.

She nodded. "I'm fine."

"Good. When was his last tetanus shot?"

"Last year," she answered automatically, anxious to go to Davey.

"Maura—" Nate hesitated. "I wouldn't make a fuss over him." He stopped her protest with three fingers across her lips. For once his eyes were absolutely devoid of their protective shuttering. They were naked, imploring her as she'd never seen Nate do before. "Please trust me on this one."

She stared at him, then managed a jerky nod. Only then did he release her and step aside, and she swept past him. She hovered over Davey for a moment, wondering what constituted fussing, wondering again what Nate knew about little boys—or perhaps just her little boy—that he apparently felt she did not.

Finally Maura picked up the broken lens and sat down next to Davey. She reached for his hand, still clasping the other half of his glasses, and drew it into her lap. For a moment, she tried to piece the glasses together, show him they could be made whole again, but it was hopeless. She gave up and squeezed his hand.

"How're you doing, son?" she asked gently, stifling the impulse to gather him into her arms and pour out the tears threatening just behind her eyes. She wanted to rage at someone—Tommy Lee, Nate, herself—for letting this happen. Why *had* it happened?

At her question, Davey had closed his eyes, as if tired. He opened them now, looking unaccountably serious with the bandage pushing one brow, and therefore the other, downward in a brooding pucker. In the light from the window, the skin around his eyes stood out in stark paleness against the tan he'd acquired in the past month. The worry line Nate had pointed out to her was fingernail deep. Davey's face, Maura noticed, wore the pinched, closed look she associated with the early days following Wayne's death. There were no tearstains on his cheeks. He stared fixedly out the window.

"I'm okay," Davey said. His gaze shifted to Nate, who'd come to stand on the other side of her, before Davey turned his head away, almost in shame. "Can I . . . can I go to bed now?"

He sounded utterly world-weary. Was it possible to feel any more heartsore or helpless than she did right now? Maura guessed he wanted not to go to bed, only to be left alone in the one place he could call his own, but he didn't feel he could ask that of her.

Susie had apparently followed Maura into the house, for now she sidled up to the bedroom door.

"I was gonna go but...can I see how Dave is?" she asked Nate.

He nodded and she approached the bed somberly. Briefly she scanned the equally somber visages of Maura and Nate before glancing at Davey.

"You okay?" she asked.

"Yeah," Davey said, surreptitiously closing the hand holding the pieces of his glasses. "Din't hurt, y'know," he averred. "Much."

"Tommy Lee is a pig!" Susie blurted out, hazel eyes flashing. "You aren't going to let him stay on the team, are ya, Coach?"

"We'll see," Nate replied ominously. He reached a hand out and gave the little girl a squeeze on the shoulder. "Thanks for fetching Maura, Susie-Q. You need a ride home?"

"Nah." Susie shrugged in an endearing, tomboyish way. "I just live down the alley." She gave Davey a loyal, almost admiring, glance. "See ya at practice tomorrow, Dave?"

Maura felt her son's hand quiver in her lap. "Prob'ly," he mumbled.

After Susie left, Nate moved to sit on Davey's other side. The three of them remained so for what seemed an eternity to Maura. With difficulty, she tried to do as Nate had asked, but it went against the grain of every maternal instinct she possessed. What she wanted to do was offer comfort—soothing words and calming touches. It would be incredibly difficult, however, to comfort the stoic, stiff little body that imprisoned her son.

What a tableau they likely made, the three of them lined up on the bed: she with her hands gripping each other to remain still; Nate hunched forward, elbows on his thighs, his hands clasped loosely between his spread knees; Davey, totem-pole straight, his own hands wrapped around his ribs. Out of the corner of her eye, she saw two profiles, mirror images of each other—darkly obscure as both Davey and Nate withdrew into themselves, containing whatever emotions they deemed too inappropriate or too volatile or too unmanly to vent.

Was this another one of those male situations she was destined never to understand completely? With her own emotions overwrought, stretched as tight as a drum, Maura wanted to scream at them.

Finally she could take the silence, the maddening inaction, no longer. "I've half a mind to go over there this minute and tell Harry and Betty Lee what I think of parents who bring their sons up to be bullies and pick fights with children younger than them."

Her son continued to stare straight ahead, lips sealed. Nate shot a glance at the boy, then met Maura's gaze over his blond head. "Not now, Maura—"

She gave him a blazingly defiant look. *Don't you dare presume to know better than me how to handle my child.* This produced sparks of anger in Nate's blue-gray eyes, but he held his counsel, with obvious effort.

"Look, honey," Maura said, disguising a caress under cover of brushing hair off Davey's forehead, "it doesn't matter what happened. We'll go to town first thing tomorrow to see about getting your glasses fixed, how about that? We'll get a brand-new pair if we have to. Maybe with different frames, would you like that? Brown ones—they call it tortoiseshell. But you can always get black again, whatever you want..."

Her voice trailed off. *Why* wouldn't he say anything? She could have handled it if he'd flung himself at her, sobbing out his anguish, his frustration or whatever it was he kept so tightly bottled within him. She'd even prefer anger from him, the kind that had made him go after Tommy, that elemental need to defend, to protect someone he loved.

Someone like Nate.

Maura stood abruptly and made a pretense of straightening the collection of miniature cars lined up on the windowsill. She blinked as a tear swelled and spilled over.

Oh God, she felt such sadness, such...regret. Yes, an immeasurable regret, bottomless as an unplumbed well. What she had feared would happen, what she'd sought to prevent had already taken place.

I'm sorry, Wayne...

Nate spoke behind her, his voice pitched low. "Where's your pj's, pard?" he asked. Davey must have shown him, for it was only a few moments before she heard the clink of a belt buckle, the thud of shoes hitting the floor.

And as he helped Davey dress for bed, Nate talked.

"You know, your dad and I got into a fight once. Of course, he wasn't your dad yet, just like your mom wasn't your mom. It was way before you were born. Anyway, we got into it, right on your mom's front porch."

"Ya did?" Clearly astounded by the prospect of Nate and his father having known each other in some unfathomable past, Davey was forced to speak. Maura noticed that Nate said nothing of Wayne attacking him. "What'd you fight about?"

"That's kind of a tough question. Do you know what you and Tommy fought about?"

Davey was silent a few minutes. That *was* a tough question for a five-year-old. Maura wondered how he'd answer.

"Tommy was callin' names," Davey said rather crossly.

"Sure, but why do you think he was calling names?"

Another stretch of silence. Maura waited.

"He was jealous, I guess, and...he just din't understand!" She heard Davey huff, apparently not happy with this explanation, either.

"You mean like those men at the barbershop didn't understand, and that made them say the things they did?"

"Sorta."

"You know, it would've been easy and a lot more satisfying that day to let 'em know what I thought of their comments," Nate said, "but I didn't see the point in stirring up the fire when I could just as well ignore it. The thing that made me maddest, though, was when they said something about my own dad—and that they said it with you standing there."

"Yeah?" Davey asked, sounding pleased that Nate regarded him so highly.

"Yup. See, I didn't want to look bad in front of you, but when I saw that you understood what they were trying to do, it didn't matter so much anymore what they said. You know? But it was real hard to walk away. In a way, even now I wish I'd said something to them, though I doubt it would've changed anyone's mind."

By now Maura had gathered that Davey had been privy to some of the talk about Nate the day he'd taken the boy to Ernie's. The pieces began to fall into place: Davey, in trying to emulate Nate, was angry with himself for letting his temper get the better of him today. But he had yet to resolve what he could have done differently once his hero had been maligned. And Nate was helping him come to terms with his actions, teaching him, as only someone who holds the position of hero can, how to be a man in the best sense of the word.

"D'ya wish you never fought my dad?" Davey asked. Maura wondered if her son knew the fight had been about her. It didn't seem to matter. Davey was obviously trying to relate more to how Nate felt about the dispute than how his father might have felt.

Nate must have discerned this and was careful in his answer. "I do—and I don't. Like most confrontations, you're in the middle of them before you realize you'd rather not be, and then it's too late. You don't know why you're there and you don't know how to get out of it. And like I said, hardly ever does it solve anything. You realize there's no use in getting into a tussle in the first place. Fighting your dad taught me that." He paused, his next words coming slowly. "We had no call, either of us, to be throwing punches for the reasons we did. But sometimes you've got to stick up for what you feel, no matter what—like your dad did."

At his words, tears filled Maura's eyes again, this time for Nate. He'd revealed none of this that night at his place, and she realized how hard it was for him to do so now. He was a man who took pride in being decisive about who he was and how he led his life. To admit ambiguity and expose himself and his actions to possible criticism went against every impulse that drove him. But he would do it for Davey.

She remembered how she'd wondered if Nate were trying to get to her through Davey and realized that even if that were not his aim, he'd done so. Her feelings for this man had grown over the past month as she got to know him, and she knew it was nothing so indiscriminate as hormones waking up after two years that drew her to him. It was his quiet sense of purpose and honor that led him to do the right thing, not only in his farming but also in his dealings with people. Even if it meant taking the shine off his own image in front of a little boy.

There were muffled noises then of clothing being doffed and donned. "Kind of funny, isn't it," Nate said, cutting the tension in the room, "how God made us with two arms and two legs situated so shirts and pants'd fit just right."

"Yeah," Davey answered. The word came out a little wobbly. Now that the threat had been confronted and diffused, he'd turned back into a child trying to suppress tears of relief that his world had survived intact. Maura cleared the lump from her throat and finally turned to face them.

Her son was crawling beneath his lariat-dappled covers as Nate wondered aloud if real cowboys slept with their spurs on.

"Not in this house, pardner." She tossed the remark off, making Davey snicker as, his composure recovered, he settled back on his pillow. *I'm learning,* she thought, though she was unable to resist bending down to give the sheet a tuck under the mattress. "How about a jelly sandwich and a glass of milk before you go to sleep?"

"Nah." Davey shook his head. "I'm not hungry."

Her son was always hungry, but she realized the effects of his first fight still lingered as she watched Davey tentatively touch the bandage on his forehead. Maura knew that whatever scar left there wouldn't serve as a trophy, as Nate had suggested. It would be a physical reminder of one of those incidents that occur in everyone's childhood, staying with them in too vivid detail for the rest of their lives. Thanks to Nate, though, in time the effects of tonight on Davey would fade much more quickly than they would have.

"Nate?" the boy asked.

"Dave?"

"Who won?"

Nate's gaze met Maura's. They both knew which altercation he meant. She had noticed how Nate had managed to bring Wayne into the conversation, make him part of the experience and part of the example for her son. She waited, eyes locked with his, to see how he would answer this question.

"Well, I don't know that anybody ever wins in a fight, because it always comes down to one person losing some self-respect, and that's never a good thing." Nate continued to hold her gaze. "But I guess if I had to call a winner in the one between me and your dad . . . your dad won."

Even if she hadn't seen it in his eyes, Maura realized how hard it was for Nate to make this admission also, though this time it wasn't because he feared seeming less to Davey. She'd never known how strongly he'd felt about that incident. Sure, he'd expressed his regret for it the evening at his house, but Maura saw now that just as she had feelings about the fight between Nate and Wayne, feelings that had yet to be confronted and resolved, so did Nate. And though he'd taken great care to avoid putting it into black-and-white terms with Davey, the fact was Nate felt he'd lost. Justly or unjustly, blamefully or not.

But if he'd lost before, his blue-gray eyes seemed to be telling her, he didn't intend to lose again.

Maura looked away first, glancing at the bedside clock. It was nearly eight-thirty. Not quite Davey's usual bedtime, but close.

She bent to give him a peck on the cheek. "Sleep tight, honey."

"G'night, Mom." He studied her, and Maura noticed how keen, almost more focused, his brown eyes seemed now than from behind his glasses. His gaze shifted to the man at her side as Maura found herself once again in the position of playing out a parent's role with Nate. "G'night, Nate."

"'Night, pardner. And thanks for sticking up for me today," he said.

The boy's face seemed to light from within at his remark. Yes, Nate had been careful not to place blame or pronounce right and wrong. Still he recognized that Davey needed the stated assurance that he'd acted correctly, and that he'd not lost Nate's regard. It was an assurance, though, only Nate could provide, as impossible for Maura to do as it would have been for Wayne. Again, regret—and guilt—assailed Maura. Then a streak of defiance shot through her. *It doesn't have to be this way.*

Nate followed her out of the room, closing the door behind him. In the narrow hallway, she turned to face him, making no effort to hide her thoughts. Surprisingly the effect was that Nate moved closer, radiating the intensity that instantly drained her resistance and made her feel so thoroughly helpless.

She couldn't prevent herself from taking one small step backward.

Even in the indistinct light, she could see Nate's chin stiffen. "Davey's glove and cap are still in the cab of my pickup," he said. "I'll go get them."

Relieved of his presence, Maura sought even more distraction. In the bathroom, she found the door to the medicine cabinet ajar. A box of bandages, also open, spilled its contents onto the vanity counter. Cotton balls sprinkled the rug.

Maura tried to return the bandages to their container, but her hands were shaking so hard she gave up after a few minutes. Like a pilgrim seeking Mecca, she found herself making her way to the kitchen, out the door and across the yard to the refuge of her garden.

She'd tended it just that morning before work. Still she searched with vigilance in the after twilight for any weed or worm that might have had the temerity to invade her dominion in the past twelve hours. Hardly realizing she did so, she murmured not only the usual words of praise she gave to her growing things but also the words of comfort she'd not been allowed to utter to Davey.

Maura heard the back door open and close, then Nate's muffled footsteps in the grass. He stopped at the edge of the garden as if held by a barrier more definite than the row of bricks.

"The carrots have upped nicely this year," she said, not looking up. "I'll have beans coming out of my ears in a week or so. You know—" she gave a little laugh "—it never fails to amaze me how you can almost see things grow. I swear this pumpkin vine gets three inches longer a day." She packed a little more mulch around the bottom of one plant. "I guess that's why I like my garden. It's always changing. When I come back to it after a few days away, it's moved on, developed on its own. It's still the same while being different. I don't know why, but I'm always amazed and surprised."

"I know what you mean," Nate said.

"It really makes you think, doesn't it?" she went on. "You become so much more aware of your place on this earth . . . that there are a lot larger forces in the world than man-made ones."

"*I know,* Maura."

"Yes, you do know what I mean. You've always known. But then we're different from other people, you and me." Her hands stilled. "And Davey. He's not the only one who takes things to heart, who wages full-scale wars within his own head as he tries to understand what's happening to him."

Placing his boots carefully between the rows of plants, Nate came to her. "I'm sorry about that fight," he said from above her. "I take it Susie told you the story?"

"Yes."

"I'm not one for explanations but I can't help thinking, after promising to look out for him, that I let you down—"

"No," Maura interrupted. "You let no one down. Nobody let anyone down." She pinched off a yellowing leaf and buried it with a certain grim satisfaction. "These things happen in little boys' lives. I don't blame you or Tommy or anyone. I...I might have thought about blaming you in the heat of the moment, but I don't now."

"That's good to know."

He was silent. She puttered, moving down the row. "It isn't easy," he said after a moment, the words seeming to be forced from him, "keeping an eye on sixteen hyper kids, trying to teach them the finer points of sportsmanship and teamwork at the same time you're teaching them to run to first base instead of third once they actually manage to hit the ball. Just like physical skills, it takes some kids longer than others to grasp character-building skills. I don't expect to work miracles, but it's durn discouraging to find out I haven't made a lick of progress with some youngsters."

Maura paused, resting her forearms on her bent knees. "What will happen to Tommy?" she asked.

"I've got the authority to kick him off the team, teach him a lesson and make an example of him for the others, but that solves my problem without doing much for Tommy." Out of the corner of her eye, she saw him toe aside the leaves of a pepper plant as he examined its progress for himself. "I'd rather try to work with him and his parents to see if there's a way he can learn a different lesson. He'd have to apologize, of course, and I'll make it clear he's got to earn the regard of his teammates and me in order to stay on the team. Who knows, though... there's only a week of Little League left. Not a lot of time to make much difference."

Nate Farrell, it seemed, did not take defeat lightly in any form.

"Well, you're certainly making a difference with Davey," she said softly. She looked up at him. "Thank you for handling him so well." She couldn't keep a certain wryness from her voice. "Much better than I could have."

His face lit much as Davey's had at the words of praise. "I'll give Davey the credit. You should be proud of the way he handled the situation. He's a good kid, real thoughtful. You're doing a great job with him."

"Despite my tendencies to mother him to death, of course." Maura brushed the dirt from her hands and stood to face him. Because she rose so quickly—or perhaps because her heart was so full and her mind so confused—her head reeled, and she put out a hand for support.

Nate's roughened palm pressed against the sensitive skin just above her elbow. He kept it there even after her vision had cleared, and though they stood in the middle of her backyard, the intimacy of his touch created a circle of privacy around them. And kept her from holding him at a distance as she so wanted to.

"Nate, you do realize this can't continue, don't you?" she said abruptly, knowing no other way to bring up the matter.

"What can't continue?"

"This growing relationship between you and Davey. It's obvious he literally worships the ground you walk on."

Nate frowned. "From what I read in the Little League handbook, a little hero worship for a coach isn't uncommon in kids. In fact, the program likes to promote that as one of its strongest benefits. Building role models aside from parents."

"But it's not just Little League," she said, frowning as well. "He's . . . getting so attached to you, Nate, and while I'm thrilled for you both, my primary responsibility has to be Davey's welfare."

She caught the flicker of his usual impassivity in his eyes, his protective mechanism, and something twisted inside her. After all he'd done for Davey, he didn't deserve this, but what option did she have?

"What are you saying, Maura?" he asked.

"Surely you can see the complications, Nate. He's going to be crushed, literally, when Tee Ball is over and he won't see you daily. When you're . . . gone."

"Gone?" Comprehension hit him. His eyes thawed with a suddenness that startled her. "But I'm not going anywhere, Maura," Nate said quietly. In fact, he moved closer as if in emphasis of his words. With bare inches between them, Maura experienced the panic she was now well acquainted with whenever Nate entered her physical sphere— except she felt it more greatly than she'd ever had before, more than the evening when he'd kissed her in the kitchen. And it was because now she knew what he wanted. Now he'd found his way into the circle of her emotions as well.

"You know what I mean," she said with a certain desperation. "You aren't...a part of our lives, not permanently. He's looking to you as a father figure."

"Is that so bad?" he asked imperturbably.

"Yes! Nate, you must see... We're friends, you and I, that's all."

"Is it, Maura?" The hand on her elbow shifted and settled at her waist, still no more than a touching, a testing, and yet the shock of it went through her like a current of electricity. What was happening was what she'd feared most.

Because it had already happened.

His thumb grazed her ribs in front; his fingers pressed her closer to him in back. Her giddiness returned. She closed her eyes to regain her equilibrium but found herself almost without a center of gravity and leaning toward him as if pulled by that infernal magnetism of his.

"Nate—"

"Maura—"

"Nate, please," she begged in a final appeal. "I feel like I'm losing...my son to you."

"You're not, Maura. I promise you that. He's growing up, changing. It's natural, and it's going to happen no matter what either of us do."

Yes, it was going to happen, no matter what she did.

With his other hand, Nate touched the back of two curled fingers to the outside of her wrist. Slowly, light as a feather, he slid his knuckles up her arm so that by the time his hand reached her throat and cupped her jaw, she was breathless, her pulse pounding against his palm. She felt the sandpapered roughness of his jaw against her temple. He nudged her with his chin and she knew that he wanted her to raise her head to look at him.

She was fraught with the warring emotions he unerringly raised in her: anticipation crashing against a buttress of self-aggravation that she had no will over her own actions. Yet the moment *had* come.

Maura lifted her chin and met Nate's eyes.

They were bottomless pools of dark blue and glinting gray, like the sun across a lake. Maura knew that look. She had been this way before, that night on her porch. She recognized the dreamlike trance as if he'd woven a spell over her.

This time there would be no interruption, no other man to break the spell, no considerate acknowledgment of her circumstances that would make Nate bow out. This time she would truly know the power of Nate Farrell.

In his own time, his own way, he'd beaten a path to the door to her heart. But still, he would ask for permission to come in. With his eyes, Nate told her it must be she who ultimately made the decision. And because of that, more than anything, she wasn't able to resist him.

Maura nodded. And Nate waited no longer. He tipped her chin a fraction higher as he bent his face to hers and covered her mouth with his.

With the same intensity that characterized Nate so well, his kiss was forceful, potent, as powerful as prayer. But gentle and giving, as well. His lips supped of hers while still returning the nourishment tenfold. Except for his hand on her waist, his finger under her chin, no other part of them touched, yet the connection was stronger than if they'd wrapped their arms about each other.

Still waters run deep, she thought through a haze. Oh, they most certainly did. They swelled and surged in complex currents; they rolled and swirled on courses ruled by a different moon entirely. And they pulled her under with the same predestination.

It was as if she'd never been kissed before—the feel of lips and teeth and tongues mingling seemed new and as exciting as it had been those first teenage years. But there was none of the unsureness of adolescence, no ineptness in the way Nate kissed her. He seemed to know, as if he'd kissed her a thousand times before, how to advance and retreat, to control the ebb and flow of sensation in a way that made Maura—a woman who was no callow youth herself, who'd experienced physical intimacy with a man—want more. So much more.

He raised his head, breaking the kiss, though their breaths still mingled.

"Is this how friends feel for each other?" he whispered.

Weakly she shook her head no.

"Then would it be out of line to suggest that it wouldn't be a trial to feel this way more often?" he asked with just the hint of a teasing smile.

She couldn't help a small chuckle. Leaning her forehead against his collarbone, she sighed. "Oh, Nate. I don't know. I get the feeling that you're looking for...for a wife," she finished, frustrated at putting it so lamely.

But Nate seemed to understand. "If that were all I was looking for, I'd be sitting in an easy chair at home right now, dandling my youngest on my knee while the little woman got the others in the tub. I can't say as I mind the prospect of a wife and family, or that I haven't had my chances over the past ten years to make my life with a few fine women. But for some reason I didn't."

His hand drifted across her cheekbone, his fingers snagging in the hair at her temple as he brushed it back, tucking it into her braid. He continued to do so in a soothing, repetitive motion. "All I know is that I want to see what the two of us could have together, now that we've been given the chance." His voice went on with that teasing note in it, "I guess I should ask first if you're going steady with someone else. I do learn from my mistakes."

Raising her head, she shook it slightly. "It's not that simple, Nate."

"How's that?"

She thought of Doreen, the expression on her face when she'd told her Nate would be taking Davey to Tee Ball practice on the days Doreen could not. She'd looked almost bleak—much as Maura remembered feeling when she had seen Davey seek Nate's touch—as if Doreen, too, wanted to set her footing just a little more strongly in the present before having to confront the future.

"I mean...people might link our names." Again she put it lamely, but it was a real concern for her, taking Doreen's feelings into consideration.

He lifted a brow at her remark. "Because your son is one of the sixteen kids I'm coaching?"

"It happened once before, you know. I didn't hear about it till later, but people were saying Drew Barnett and I were a couple, all because he dropped by once in a while to see how I was doing."

His hand stilled. "I remember that. And it taught me just how much credence to put into gossip. After all, look what came of it—Drew married Callie. But I still don't see the point in all this."

"It's the same point as with Davey," she explained. "He's liable to think...things, too. I have to take that into account."

Nate tugged her close as his palm cupped the back of her head. "Somehow I don't think it's Davey's welfare or the town's gossip that's the problem here." Closer still...those blue-gray eyes of his mesmerizing. She felt herself slipping again under the spell.

"No," he murmured, "Davey pretty much proved today that he can take care of himself. And as far as the town's concerned, I'm ready to really give them something to talk about."

This time there was no invitation. He pulled her into his arms, laid her head against his shoulder and kissed her. And,God help her, she kissed him back. One hand slid up his back, so firm and solid, while she rested her other hand against that broad chest of his.

Nate groaned. His lips moved over hers possessively, as if he knew what it would take to blot out her reservations. And yet Maura knew he still restrained himself, perhaps doubting his own strength or doubting she was ready for that strength.

How much more could there be? The question set off a quivering deep inside her that radiated outward from her core, until she shook like a leaf in his arms.

Again he broke the kiss and clasped her tightly against his chest to still her shuddering. She clung to him despite herself.

"Tell me, Maura," he spoke into her hair, urging her. "Tell me what you're afraid of."

She shook her head against his shoulder. What would she say, that it was him, the very definition of him, asking for and expecting everything of himself and others, that frightened her? *You're just too intense.*

There was an irresistible power in that intensity Maura had long recognized. Had his nature been different, Nate Farrell would have been one of those dangerous men whom women with any sense avoided, even while they experienced a kind of dissatisfaction with themselves for not taking up the challenge of such a compelling life force.

How different would her life have been had she done so those years ago? Maura wondered. If she'd devastated Wayne Foster, defied her father, made the choice to love Nate Farrell in the all-or-nothing way he demanded...? How could a girl *not* rise to such a challenge, especially at an untried age when anything was still possible? Why hadn't she? It occurred to Maura that this was why she'd blocked that incident from her memory. She'd recognized the kind of man Nate was. Had she been given the opportunity, she could have explored her attraction to Nate. But she hadn't been given that opportunity. She'd been forced to choose— him or Wayne.

And that was what she feared: having no choice. Where Nate was concerned, she had no control over her actions. And it felt as if she had no control over her life.

When she made no answer, Nate drew away from her a little, his gaze now gentle, though within its depths she could see he was struggling with his own reservations. "Look, Maura, I don't want the world from you—"

Oh yes, you do, she almost replied. *You always have and you always will.*

The thought must have shown on her face, for his eyes glinted suddenly, reservations falling away in that dangerous way she'd pinpointed seconds before. "And I'm not going to eat you up, although—" he dipped his head and nipped her lower lip in a way wholly unlike the Nate she knew, and wholly thrilling "—the notion has its appeal. All I want is a chance," he whispered against her mouth. "Give me that."

A chance. A choice. It was all both of them wanted, she realized. All that anyone wanted—and deserved. She thought of Davey, struggling with so much, taking the world on his small shoulders because he didn't know he had an option of doing it another way. Nate himself, facing so much more than financial depletion should his changeover to organic farming produce anything less than the best results, yet knowing he had to take the risk. They labored as she labored, hoped as she hoped. They were growing and learning, like she was, and making their way. And making their choices. To deny them a chance would be like denying her own efforts to go on with her life.

And suddenly a need rose up in her. She deserved that chance.

Maura slid out of Nate's arms. "Where do people go on dates these days?" she asked.

He shifted on his feet. "I'd be pleased if you and Davey would join me on the Fourth a week or so from now. We could watch the parade, drive out to my folks' for dinner before we take in the carnival at the park."

"The Fourth?" she echoed. He would pick that day. Accompanying Nate to the Fourth of July celebration implied all the things that going with him to homecoming or prom would have signified in high school.

"Or some other time," he said. "It's up to you, Maura."

Yes, it was her choice. She must always remember that she had a choice.

"The Fourth sounds fine," she replied. "I'd like to spend part of the day with Doreen and Kenny. Davey will want to, too."

There was a flicker of acknowledgment in his eyes as he nodded. "I'll call you." He hesitated, and the kisses they'd shared, the concessions on both sides that had come out of those kisses, lingered between them. Maura realized she wanted him to take her in his arms again so she could feel her doubts melt away as they had before. But Nate only touched her arm in a brief parting before he turned and left.

Maura made her way back to the darkened house. She washed up and wiped down the already pristine counter. Hands now rock steady, she straightened the bathroom. On the way back to her room, she paused outside Davey's door. Grasping the knob, she cracked the door open.

His head turned on the pillow. "Mom?"

"You still awake?" She perched on the edge of the bed, next to him. "Does your head hurt?"

He nodded. She got him a children's pain reliever and a glass of water. He gulped it noisily, then admitted that a little something to eat would not be declined. She made him a sandwich, which he ate while she waited. They chatted of inconsequential matters, and she listened, anticipating the inevitability of Davey's relating everything back to Nate. But the boy didn't mention his name, for once.

"All done?" Maura said when the last crust of bread had disappeared. She took the plate as he scooted under the covers. It was on the tip of her tongue to mention brushing his teeth, but she decided one night wouldn't hurt. He could have used a bath, too. No matter. She knew better than to ask if he wanted her to lie down beside him for a while and so was surprised and pleased when he made the request himself.

It was only after she'd snuggled him up against her and inhaled the tangy smell of little-boy hair that she suspected Davey had asked for this comfort not for himself but for her. Still he sighed, a complete release of tension, and she felt the tension leave her, as well.

"You've had quite a day, haven't you, Davey boy?" she murmured.

"Yeah."

Moments passed, and Maura thought he'd drifted off when he spoke up suddenly. "I don't want to be Davey anymore, Mom."

Alarm raced through her at the contradictory statement. "What do you mean, son?"

"I want to be Dave."

"I see." And she was no longer Mama—just Mom. He was growing up, just as Nate said. "Would it be all right, though, if I still called you Davey when it's just you and me?"

He mulled this over.

"All right," he answered. "I guess if you really wanna, you could call me that even when it's not just you an' me. But maybe not 'honey,' okay, Mom?" he negotiated the compromise.

"Okay." She could live with that if he could.

Maura pressed her lips to the top of his head. "Good night, my dear, sweet son."

Chapter Six

The Fourth of July dawned clear and warm and right on schedule, despite Davey's doubts.

"I thought it'd *never* come," he told Maura and Doreen that morning as they walked the few blocks to Main Street to watch the parade.

"Did you think we'd pass right over it, like February 29th?" Doreen asked.

Davey looked up at his grandmother, his clear brown eyes no longer obscured behind lenses. Maura noticed, as she had more and more in the past week, how much her son did resemble her.

What had happened was nothing short of a minor miracle. Since he'd been due for an eye checkup around the time he'd broken his glasses, Maura took him to the doctor before getting a replacement pair. The news had been that, with Davey's devotion to wearing his lenses, the focusing problem that had remained after his operation had straightened itself out. He no longer needed glasses.

The effect on the boy was akin to watching a flower open. At first he held his feelings close in, but once he ventured a look around and realized that he could see perfectly fine, he'd blossomed and become very nearly a different boy altogether. Maura, with a developing vision of her own, suspected the change was due to more than discarding a pair of plastic glasses. If he were flourishing, it was because of careful and constant nurturing. Though Maura could give herself some of the credit, she knew a certain man had been just as great an influence on her son. And she lost a little more of her heart to Nate Farrell.

Davey's brow puckered at Doreen's question. "You mean there's a day that gets left out?"

"Except during leap year, then they count it."

"Do they just forget it when they're making up calendars?" Walking between the adults, he turned to Maura for assurance, clearly appalled by the gross negligence of "them." "But they couldn't! What if they forgot Halloween or Easter or—or *Christmas?*"

"February 29th is the only day that's ever skipped," Maura said, maintaining a straight face only by avoiding Doreen's eyes. "They add it in once every four years because..." How did she put it into terms a five-year-old could understand? "It's called Sadie Hawkins' Day—the only day the girls get to do the proposing to the boy they like best, so you see they couldn't have it every year."

"Oh." Either her explanation was adequate or Davey didn't consider the exclusion of Sadie Hawkins' Day, and therefore a dearth in unwanted proposals, a big loss to humanity. He gave a little hop as his excitement returned. "Nate's going to take me on the Ferris wheel this afternoon," he announced in an awed tone at his own daring. "After my dinner settles a'course. I don't wanna have it all come right back up again."

This time the two women couldn't hold back their laughter, even as Maura felt her cheeks flush. She didn't need to see the mind wheels turning to know how Davey had come

up with the change in subject from favored beaus to Nate.
Obviously her own excitement about the significance of this
day had not been lost on Davey.

But it was the first time Nate's name had come up between the two women since she'd called Doreen to work out
the schedule for the day. She, Davey and Doreen would
watch the parade together. Then Maura and Davey would
have lunch with Nate's family before they returned to town
and took in the carnival and the rest of the celebration. Doreen would have her grandson for supper, the fireworks and
overnight while Nate and Maura went to the pig roast and
street dance on Main. The two women had discussed the
logistics matter-of-factly, and Maura had gotten the feeling
that Doreen was making an effort to remain carefully neutral—if she weren't exactly glad to see her daughter-in-law
dating, still, she realized it wouldn't be unusual for Maura
to do so after two years.

It was the kind of support Maura needed most. She knew
how hard it was for Doreen, just as it was for her, to think
about moving on, and Maura didn't expect wholehearted
backing. She respected her mother-in-law for her restraint
in letting Maura feel her own way, and it made her love the
older woman even more.

Just so, nothing seemed amiss in Doreen's smile as she
told Davey, "Well, if you do get a little shook up, I've heard
a scoop of homemade ice cream is just the thing for a wobbly tummy."

"Homemade ice cream!"

"You betcha. Two kinds. So don't eat too much of the
candy that's thrown out at the parade. Your Uncle Kenny
said he was going to look for you and make sure you got a
whole bunch."

The expression on Davey's face was one of dazed disbelief at being the recipient of such a wealth of good fortune.
Maura squeezed the small hand she held in hers. Oh, to be
a child again, to have that sense of discovery, to take such
pleasure in the small things, like Ferris wheels and parades

and homemade ice cream. And yet a kindred anticipation had infected her, as well. Now that the day was indeed here, she found herself impatient as Davey to commence the festivities. To see Nate again.

But first she had the parade to get through. It was an enjoyable, informal affair, with much calling back and forth of greetings and good-natured insults between participants and spectators. Otie Slater, Soldier Creek's mayor, went by in a mint-condition Thunderbird on loan from one of the gearheads in town. The pork, beef and lamb queens, having images to maintain, duly ignored the wolf whistles and impudent invitations from the young men in the crowd. Each club and organization had a float—a flatbed wagon draped in crepe paper on which various townspeople depicted an animated slice of pioneer life. Though, to be sure, there were breaks in character as the players encountered familiar faces on the parade route and waved.

Then came the procession of farm equipment, large and impressive as mastodons: combines and four-wheel-drive tractors, one hauling a planter with as many as twenty-four bottoms. They shone bright as beacons in the morning sun—kelly green with yellow emblems, or fire-engine red.

In a way, it occurred to Maura, some of that equipment really was heading the way of the extinct mastodon. At least, it would if Nate's way of farming caught on in any significant fashion. Quality would take precedence over quantity. And the indiscriminate use of chemicals, used in greatest quantity in row crops, would be considered irresponsible in the nineties. More and more, people were beginning to hold farmers accountable for what they did to the land and environment, much as was happening in other industries around the country.

To some of the older farmers, Maura realized, such change would spell more than a new way of farming. They would lose the connection they had with their own fathers, never to regain it. Perhaps that's what they resisted. Not change, but a finality. The end of a way of life, the only one they'd ever known.

"There's Uncle Kenny!" Davey cried.

Maura shaded her eyes against the sun. High up, a blond-haired man leaned out of the cab of a combine, laughing as he tossed a handful of candy into the crowd. For a split second, it seemed she was looking at Wayne. Lean and lanky, Kenny was a younger version of his brother, with Wayne's same blithe temperament, which made Kenny so good at the job that took him all over the Midwest selling farm implements.

It had been some time since she'd seen Wayne's brother, who set down roots in Newton when he wasn't traveling. And as she watched his gaze light on them, and Davey's jubilation as Kenny swung down from the cab and singled his nephew out of the crowd for a special treat, Maura felt an odd blend of regret and guilty relief. At one time, she'd wished Kenny didn't travel so much, in the hopes that he'd provide the male companionship Davey lacked. Now, though, seeing how well Davey got along with Nate, she was glad the opportunity had never come up. Kenny could never handle Davey as intuitively as Nate could.

The judgment popped into her head from nowhere, surprising her. But it was true. At twenty-five, Kenny still lacked a certain maturity that she'd have thought the deaths of two male family members would produce in him.

"So, Davey boy," he was saying now, "your aim improved much from last year? I'm not taking any nephews to the baseball toss who still can't hit the broad side of a barn."

"I'm lots better than last year," Davey bragged as he dug into the large paper bag Kenny held and came out with a fistful of Tootsie Rolls. "I been practicing!"

His uncle cuffed him affectionately. "Go on with ya."

"Uh-huh. Nate says I'm good enough to dunk him at the dunking machine."

The smile died on Kenny's face. His gaze shot to Doreen in surprise, then to Maura, then back to Doreen.

"Nate Farrell has asked Maura and Davey to spend the day with him and his family," Doreen spoke up. "Wasn't that nice of him?"

Maura thought Doreen would have told Kenny about their plans before this. Obviously she hadn't. But there was more than surprise in his gaze. Maura was taken aback by the betrayal that virtually leapt out at her, and Kenny looked inclined to pass comment on Nate's "niceness" when a shout distracted him.

"Hey, Foster, the natives are gettin' hungry!" The parade had moved on, and dozens of children waited their turn to scramble for a piece of candy.

"Comin' right up!" Kenny announced, raising his arm and dousing the nearby section with a spray of Tootsie Rolls. He turned back to Davey with a doting smile. "I got a buck in quarters for the kid who thinks he can put a baseball through the ring and win a prize."

"Okay!" Davey said.

"And I've got your favorite for dinner, fried chicken and potato salad," Doreen informed Kenny, catching his eye significantly.

He gave her that winning Foster smile, as well. "I've got to help set up chairs at the band shell, and I'll be over," he told her.

Then, without a parting word or even glance at Maura, he turned and ambled off.

Maura smoothed the front of her sundress for the tenth time and told Davey to come away from the front window for the nineteenth. Nate was to pick them up here to take them out to his parents' for lunch. Her stomach was so fluttery she wondered if she'd be able to eat a bite, and then if that would insult Sally Farrell unforgivably. She worried about Davey's behavior; the Farrells weren't used to children. And she pondered on Kenny's—there had been something quite obdurate in his expression that also kept wings beating against her diaphragm. Finally she abandoned Davey to his own devices and went to the bathroom where she washed the perspiration from her palms.

In the mirror, she checked her hair, also for the tenth time. She'd tried something new, a French braid, and was glad to see it was holding. To the end of it she'd tied a sage-colored ribbon that matched her cloth belt. Her dress, new as well, was a deep, dusky mauve in a cool cotton. Nervously she fingered the scoop neckline then, twisting her arm behind her, touched the portion of spine revealed by the diamond-shaped cutout in the back of the dress. Also new and quite daring for Maura.

Was the dress too fancy? Too fussy? Too obvious?

"He's here!" Davey yelled in case she didn't hear the sound of a vehicle pulling into the driveway, a motor shutting off. Heavy male footsteps resounded on the wooden porch before she heard a rap on the door.

"I'll get it!" her son volunteered, as if he weren't standing right there.

Maura stepped into the hall as Nate entered. Their gazes met and clung.

As always, he filled her house, seemed to take it over, he was so tall and broad through the chest. He wore a pair of lightweight pleated trousers, in a fashionable tan shade, that fit his slim waist to a T, and a light blue camp shirt, open at the throat. He looked so different, like someone out of a magazine, and she realized he'd put some thought into his attire, as well. Today, without his usual cap, his mahogany hair shone in its full burnished glory as it curled at his temple. She found herself almost memorizing his features—that fine, straight nose, the fascinating cleft in his chin—as they stared at each other, he still at the doorway, she still with a towel in her hands halfway down the hall. They could have been the only two people in the world.

His incredible eyes shone from his tanned face like star sapphires. With a slow thoroughness, Nate took in every detail of her appearance, as well, in a way that told her that she wasn't too fancy, too fussy, too obvious. As far as he was concerned, she was just right.

"Hello, Maura," he said after a moment.

Maura smiled as the wings that had been beating against the walls of her chest finally found a roost and calmed their ruffled feathers. "Hello, Nate."

"Nate!" Davey said impatiently.

With the effect of being tugged away, his glance eventually settled on the boy at his side. She and Nate must have been staring at each other for over a minute, Maura realized.

"Hey there, pard," Nate said with a ruffling of blond hair, giving the boy what Maura had come to think of as Davey's special look. "Ready to get the show on the road, are you?"

"You betcha. I got four whole dollars saved up to spend."

"And I'll wager it's burning a hole in your pocket, isn't it?"

"No way. Mom's keeping it in her purse for me so I won't zackcidently lose it."

Nate laughed, turning to Maura, and she found herself suddenly without a breath. With his eyes and face lit up like that and not a trace of his usual reserve, she glimpsed just how truly handsome a man Nate Farrell could be. For the first time in her life, she wished her son were somewhere else, just for a few minutes.

Nate held out his hand to her, and she moved to take it as if it were the most natural gesture in the world. Her other hand she offered to Davey. He took it and, also quite naturally, slipped his other hand into Nate's. They stood like that for a moment—man, woman and child in a circle of completion—and again Maura saw Davey shake his head as if he couldn't believe this was happening to him. That he could be so happy.

He asked for so little, this dear son of hers, and it was because he believed that so much of what he wanted was out of his reach. Yes, he craved material things—barber cuts and baseball gloves and homemade ice cream. But what he wanted most was to feel able to love and be loved without restriction. Without the fear of loss. He wanted to look forward to the future again. And if this man could restore such faith in her child, it would take a better woman than she to deny either of them that opportunity.

They walked to Nate's truck with Davey between them. And when Maura glanced at Nate over her son's head, she knew that Davey wasn't the only one who'd rediscovered hope through Nate Farrell.

Sally Farrell made Maura feel right at home by putting her to work. Nate's mother gave her the task of arranging vegetables and assorted relishes on a lazy Susan while Sally bustled about seeing to the final touches of dinner. Nate and Davey were banished to the front porch, where Nate's father was already holding forth in exile.

Maura didn't know Nate's mother very well but found her to be a no-nonsense individual fully capable of running a busy country inn. She saw where Nate got his reserve, for though Sally was welcoming, the older woman maintained a friendly distance. As they chatted about inconsequential subjects, Maura soon spotted a thread running through their conversation that told her Sally Farrell was as protective of her quiet son as Maura was of her own. Obviously, to Sally, Maura was a potential threat to her son's happiness, and it made her wonder what the older woman knew about the incident with Nate and Wayne.

After Nate's sister and her husband arrived, the atmosphere cleared as Callie kept up a running chatter about a million different things as she, too, hustled around the kitchen with purpose.

"Wouldn't Dad enjoy helping us, too?" she asked half a dozen times until Sally scolded her.

"Don't you dare call your father in here. It's hard enough as it is to keep him on his low-cholesterol diet without putting temptation at his fingertips.'' She popped an olive into her mouth on her way past Maura.

Duly chastised, Callie was silent only a second before she burst out, "Pavlova's with foal again,'' speaking of the mare she kept, along with Drew's stallion and the yearling that had already been produced, at the Barnett homestead. "I hope it'll be a filly this time.''

"I wondered why I didn't see you riding her in the parade,'' Maura commented.

"Oh, I could still ride her for several months yet,'' Callie said, "but the veterinarian here says I'm not allowed.'' Saucily she glanced at Drew, who for some reason had dared to remain in his mother-in-law's domain instead of joining the men. He leaned against the counter, the heels of his hands propped on either side of him, and well out of anyone's way. Even if Maura hadn't seen the way his gaze followed Callie around the room, she'd have to have been blind not to spot the exclusive look that now passed between them.

Sally, whose back had been turned, didn't catch on. "Now, Drew. Far as I know it never hurt a mare to keep active right up to the time she foaled,'' she said, then turned a becoming shade of pink, as if just realizing she no longer spoke to the boy who'd grown up alongside her own, but a man who was now a professional in his own right.

"Well, Sally, I have to agree,'' Drew said diplomatically. "Most brood mares know their limits—''

"Brood mare!'' Callie sputtered on a laugh.

"—but there're some fillies, first time around, who need a firm but gentle hand to keep them in line.''

"I realize Pavlova would've been skittish in her first pregnancy,'' Sally allowed, "but you think she'll be so this time?''

"Oh, Pavlova'll be fine, I imagine. Although I've learned the female gender in general is an unpredictable lot. Tetchy, too. You've got to be on your toes with them. One minute a filly will be as peaceful as a lamb, and the next she'll be taking a chunk out of your hide.''

"That's right," Callie retorted. "I'd watch my back if I were you, Drew Barnett!"

Maura laughed with Drew while Sally still looked confused. "What are you kids talking about?"

"Oh, Mom," Callie sighed, and gave her mother a huge smile. "Pavlova's not the only one expecting."

Sally looked momentarily stunned, then clapped her hands delightedly and opened her arms to Callie. Hugs and congratulations were being distributed all around when Nate walked in.

"Who won the lottery in here?" he asked.

"Callie's going to have a baby!" Sally said, grandmotherly pride springing full grown from her breast. She hurried from the room to fetch her husband and let him in on the celebration.

Maura watched Nate's expression soften into a look of extraordinary tenderness as he enfolded his sister in his arms.

"Way to go, kiddo," he said into her hair as he rocked her.

"Oh, Nate," she choked, clinging to him and crying tears of joy as she hadn't even within her mother's embrace. But Maura recognized them as tears of relief, as well. The two of them, brother and sister, had been through much over the past eighteen months as they took over the house and farm to help out their parents. They'd suffered some pretty discouraging setbacks in the process. This event, more than any other, signified that the Farrell family would go on with a certainty.

Still holding Callie against his side, Nate extended a hand to his friend. Drew grasped it firmly as an uncontrollable grin overtook his face.

"Way to go, too, *stud,*" Nate teased wickedly.

"Nate!" Callie punched him in the chest while the tips of Drew's ears grew red.

"Let's see who's next, *friend,*" he replied, cocking a brow significantly.

Nonplussed, Maura felt herself blush. Three pairs of blue eyes focused on her, a different expression in each: Drew's, a pure blue, were kindly speculative and approving; Callie's, the same blue-gray as her brother's, were speculative also, with the same concern Maura had glimpsed in Sally's gaze.

Then she found Nate's eyes and couldn't look away. It occurred to her that she had felt a twinge of envy standing there as she watched Callie glow with her wonderful secret, knowing what grew within her. And Maura realized that she hadn't thought about having other children for a long, long time. Once she'd taken it for granted she and Wayne would have more. Yet when he died, she hadn't mourned the loss of those unconceived children. Neither, though, had she dwelt upon the possibility of having them with another man, and she knew now it was because she hadn't allowed herself to. Struggling to hold constant the present had taken up all of her energies.

But now, within Nate's eyes, Maura found something to make her look ahead, to think about the possibilities that lay in the uncharted future that just weeks ago had seemed so daunting.

"Callie! Drew!" Sally's voice carried to them from the front of the house. "Come on out here so Dad can give you a hug!"

As a result of the good news, dinner was an even more boisterous affair. Davey, disconcerted by so many strangers, was quiet until Nate's father drew him out by making such outrageous statements—"I hear tell you hit three home runs ever' time you get up to bat"—that Davey, in all honor, had to refute them. He caught on quickly, though, dissolving into fits of laughter as Oran escalated each assertion. Soon Nate, Callie and Drew joined in, asking how Davey could permit such inventions to go uncorrected.

As the meal progressed, Maura learned that the Farrells liked to tease, and that Nate and his father were the worst of the bunch.

The bond ran deeply between father and son. Despite Nate's concerns that his changes around the farm had adversely affected his father, Maura could see that Oran understood, perhaps more than Nate himself realized, the commitment his son had undertaken, and he was proud of Nate. In fact, Maura reasoned, Oran Farrell was a very smart man. By supporting Nate's ambitions, he was holding on to his son at a time when more and more young men were deciding that carrying on the family farm was not for them.

"Wait," Nate said in a low voice as she rose to help clear the table when they were finished eating. "I've got something to show you."

Maura glanced with concern toward Davey, but he seemed to have overcome any shyness and was trotting after Oran, who apparently had something to show him, too.

She smiled at Nate, glad to steal a few unexpected moments of privacy. "What've you got?" she asked.

He said nothing but led her outside, across the backyard and beyond the barn and outbuildings. A path had been carved through the high grass, and the ground sloped downward the farther they went. It was quite a hike in the middle of a hot July day, but Maura didn't mind as soon as she realized their goal.

To the uneducated eye, it would have looked like a neglected, overgrown and rather damp pasture. This was Nate's marsh. A "prairie pothole," he explained, that, though it would be years before it actually achieved true marsh status, was important now for its shallowness—swales with water even one inch deep were the first to thaw in the spring and get the food chain stirring. Once this did become a marsh, he told her, an acre of such land could clean runoff from one hundred acres in the right situation.

They talked little as they wandered about. Occasionally Nate would point out something to her, how the milkweed or sunflowers, weeds reviled by conventional farmers, were doing well, how he'd found the nest of a rare upland sandpiper over there. Afterward they strolled back toward the house, again with nary a word between them, but it was an easy silence she didn't want to end.

On the far side of the barn, she paused to shake a pebble out of her sandal and wondered how to prolong their time alone. Nate's thoughts were apparently running along the same lines, for when she straightened, her shoulder bumped against his forearm as his hand braced against the faded red barn.

She made a small noise of apology, then looked up into his eyes. They were a burning blue, and they burned purposefully into her, making her feel within seconds like melted butterscotch inside.

His other hand came up to brush her cheek. "I didn't get the chance to tell you how pretty you look in that dress," he said huskily.

She felt herself blush under the heat of his gaze. "I made it, you know," she said inanely. Her hand went to her neckline, not excessively revealing but rather low cut for her.

"Mmm. You look like a rose in it, all fresh and pink and glowing." Slowly his eyes wandered over her, which had the effect of making her pinker and more glowing. "Or maybe some kind of confection. Mom makes this fluffy candy around the holidays that looks like clouds—"

"Divinity," Maura supplied in an insubstantial voice.

"Divinity," he concurred, letting the word roll off his tongue. "She tints it with something—"

"Food coloring," she again interrupted in an even fainter voice.

"—some pieces the very shade of pink in your cheeks. You know what I like about divinity?"

"Wh-what?" she asked, becoming mesmerized by his voice, and wilder with expectation than she would have thought she could be in so little time.

"It just seems to... melt in your mouth."

He bent his face to hers, and Maura closed her eyes in anticipation of his kiss. But she felt his lips beneath her ear, nuzzling upward, tasting the tender lobe in a way that made her draw in her breath with effort.

"You can't eat much of the stuff, that's for sure," he went on, his thumb caressing her other earlobe as his fingers slid into the hair at her nape. "One little piece, that's all, because it's so sweet..."

His mouth drifted across her jawline, his teeth issuing little nips along the way. Finally his lips found hers and sealed them with a brief, succulent kiss. When she pressed closer for more, he drew away with a flick of his tongue across the sensitive bow of her upper lip.

"Don't, Nate," Maura said, sounding sulky even to her own ears, but she was thoroughly frustrated—though thoroughly captivated—with the way he teased her. A turbulence was building inside her that she'd never experienced before, making her yearn to meet its force.

"Don't what?" he asked against her mouth. His hand slid lower, stroking her throat, feathering across her collarbone, covering her hand, as it lay over her pounding heart, with his.

Her head spun with his nearness. "Don't... tease." She reached for him, dug her fingers into the solid muscle of his shoulder. His breath quickened against her cheek.

"But I like to tease," he whispered as the hand that had been propped against the barn coasted down her back.

"It's not nice," Maura managed, as if she were scolding Davey. Nate's fingers found the diamond of exposed flesh and spread against her spine. "It just isn't, sometimes—"

"Ah, but sometimes it's not meant to be nice," he muttered, and finally melded his mouth to hers. His splayed hand brought her hard against him, and she wrapped her arms around his neck and drank in his kiss, absorbing him like sun-parched soil soaks up rain.

Oh, yes, Nate Farrell was a shameless tease. And she was shameless in her response, losing herself in him as she once feared she would and now could not imagine doing without. She wanted this, desperately wanted him. She knew she had to be falling in love, but how could that be, when she'd never felt this way before?

No, this was all brand-new and wondrous, this discovery that he could inspire such passion in her.

But at the same time it shocked her. *He* shocked her, with his purposeful seduction that she couldn't *not* respond to. His intensity, when he turned it on her, demanded response. If he hadn't known before how little control she had over herself when with him, he did now. The thought called forth the fear that had shaken her to her core from the first time he'd taken her in his arms, and it made her tremble anew.

"Maura," Nate rasped in agony, taking her face between his hands. "What is it, sweet? I can't stand to see you so frightened. Tell me."

"It's you," she said, her voice alarmed. "You—and me. Oh, Nate, you make me feel so . . . so out of control. So easily. I don't know myself. I . . . I don't know you, when you tease me so."

He drew back slightly. "Are you afraid I don't mean it, that I'm playing with you?" he asked quietly.

"No, I didn't mean like that. I just don't know what it is, this . . . this power you have over me."

His eyes were the color of violets in sunlight. "Don't you, Maura? It's the same power you hold over me, that makes me lure you out by the barn so I can have a minute alone with you, to touch you and kiss you like I've been dying to for a week."

She shook her head in confusion. "It's like some game," she tried again.

"It *is* a game, Maura—a wonderful, playful game, just between us two."

"But I don't know the rules!"

He went still, his gaze probing hers. "What are you saying?"

"Don't you think I wish I knew?" she asked on a choked laugh that ended in a groan. "This is all so new, completely different from—"

She broke off, struck by what she'd been about to say, knowing it had struck Nate, as well. For once the comparison stopped there, as if a door closed behind her and she no longer had the option of looking back from whence she came. At least not in this realm of just the two of them, where Nate was so real and alive. There could be no room for anything or anyone else but him in her mind—and in her heart.

Solemnly she raised her eyes to his. Touched his face with her fingertips. "Would you believe me if I told you I've never felt this way before?"

"Never?"

She looked at him steadily. "Never."

He smiled then as he had this morning, breathtakingly, though there was an even greater brilliance that seemed to fill him, making his blue-gray eyes incandescent with fantastic highlights that stole any reason she might still have had.

"Oh, Maura, what have you missed?" he sighed roughly. "What have I . . . ?"

He crushed her to him, kissed her with a surety that his kisses hadn't held before. She strove to meet him, to provide him with her own assurances that *yes, this is right, this is more than right.* It was like trying to grasp the nature of divinity, real divinity: the notion that there existed a force that not only had no end, but no beginning, either. Likewise, the connection between this man and her had always existed.

And she wanted it never to end; Nate's mouth rejected any end. The rasp of his beard, the velvet of his tongue over her lips, made them ever more sensitive, ever more responsive. Maura gloried in the hard feel of him against her softness, marveled at the way they fit together. But then, all of nature was so. Where there was a furrow, there were seeds to fill it. Where there were cool valleys, there were sun-kissed peaks to shade their lushness.

Everything works together, but only if everything is pledged to that end.

"Sweet," Nate murmured, loosening his hold on her but still keeping her close. "That's what I'll call you."

"I wondered when you'd come up with a nickname for me." She cast her gaze down in a flirting pout, loving that she could do so with him. "I mean, Davey's 'pardner,' Callie's 'kiddo'—"

"Yes, but I wouldn't call her that if she didn't hate it so much."

Maura smiled, then remembered she was supposed to be pouting. "Even Susie Henderson has a nickname."

"Don't forget Drew's," he reminded her roguishly.

Neither could stifle their laughter.

"So do I get a nickname?" he asked. "Aside from Crazy Nate, that is. Although—" he bent his head and nuzzled her ear with his nose, blowing out softly as a horse might and sending a cascade of goose bumps down her arm "—it would depend on the situation. I'm definitely feeling a little crazy right now."

Maura dug her fingers into his hair and pressed his cheek to hers as sudden tears stung behind her eyes. Just a few months ago, she'd seen this man's face turn to stone at the mention of that name. Now, though, things had changed, so that he could joke about it. And it was because Nate had found understanding. With her, through her, in her. For that she felt profoundly thankful, yet Nate wasn't the only one who'd found understanding and had changed as a result.

Much like Davey, she'd blossomed and grown. All three of them had.

"Do you think," she asked when she could control her voice, "if I spread it around, people might start calling you Wise and Sensible Nate?"

"Doesn't have quite the same ring, does it?" he asked tenderly, giving her a squeeze. "You *are* sweet, Maura," he whispered against her temple. "Sweeter than divinity... sweeter than heaven."

Sweet. Not a nickname but an endearment, as much of one as Nate might ever utter and, because of that, so much more expressive than "darling" or "dear" could ever be. Words of love, of any kind, would never spring freely from his lips; he wasn't that kind of man. Never, though, would a person doubt the words he did say.

She looked up at him shyly. "Sometimes you can be so...eloquent, Nate."

He looked stunned. This was obviously not a description he would have applied to himself, though he seemed pleased. Then he raised his brows in doubt. "*Eloquent* Nate?"

They stared at each other, then burst out laughing, these two people to whom laughter had never come easily.

But then they *had* missed so much.

"There you two are!"

Nate and Maura had returned to the yard and just rounded the side of the house. Davey stood on the front porch, arms akimbo, fists on his waist, in a perfect imitation of Maura.

"I been lookin' all over for you!" he said as they approached.

"We took a little walk to settle our dinners," she explained, mounting the steps and giving her son a squeeze around the shoulders in apology. He'd probably been half crazy thinking about all the action going on at the carnival without him. But the boy didn't seem angry, just impatient. Maura managed to keep her fingers from brushing across her swollen lips and calling more attention to them. Davey gave her a suspicious glance anyway before scrutinizing Nate, who grinned unrepentantly from the foot of the steps.

Davey's irritation fell away as he held out his hand to Maura. "Lookit I found, Mom," he said. Over a dollar in change lay in his palm.

"Davey!" Maura was shocked. "Where on earth did you get that money?"

"I told ya. I found it, most of it in the yard."

She turned puzzled eyes to Nate, who in turn gave his father, who sat next to Sally on the porch swing, a reproving glance. Oran shrugged inculpably.

"Say, Dave," Nate said, "why don't you go on in and wash your hands before we head into town? You might want to spruce up a bit—I mean, Susie Henderson mentioned that she'd be in line to get me at the dunking machine."

Davey's face was speculative as he brushed his fingers over his cowlick. Then, whistling, he banged into the house in search of water and a comb.

"So where'd he get that money?" Maura asked, crossing her arms and arching an eyebrow at Nate.

"Well," he began, hiking the leg up on his trousers and setting the ball of his foot on an upper step as he crossed his forearms on his thigh, "before dinner I was sitting on the swing there and some change slipped out of one of these pockets. Davey noticed it first, and he was just so tickled I didn't have the heart to say anything.... Besides, finder's keepers. You know."

He shot his father a provoked look. Oran continued to swing gently, watching his son as if he were awaiting elucidation as much as Maura.

"I see," she said, getting the picture. "And then?"

"Then—and I'm guessing here—after dinner Davey somehow got the notion that there was more money to be found and, taking a few hints from someone who should know, he ran around the yard discovering change about the way you find eggs on Easter morning."

"Ah," Maura said, "so is this what you mean when you tell me the Farrells are growing some alternative crops?"

"You bet," Oran finally spoke up, given that opening. "Best 'cash' crop around."

Sally rolled her eyes tolerantly, having seen thirty-some years of such puns.

"Well, I think this is just wonderful." Maura smiled sweetly all around. "Up to now, all Davey's been able to find in our yard is a single Indian-head nickel, even after digging a two-foot-deep hole. With the idea planted in his head, imagine what he'd find here with a little effort and a decent shovel."

The porch swing ground to a halt. Sally fixed first her son, then her husband, with a rebuking eye. "If I find craters in my lawn next week, 'twon't be that child that takes a licking. And, mind you, I've still got strength in this arm!"

Maura entered the house on dwindling laughter as she went to fetch her purse and freshen up a little herself. She found Callie in one of the bedrooms, standing at the window gazing out, her arms wrapped around her.

Callie turned as she heard Maura come in behind her. She didn't need to ask what Callie had been thinking about.

"I enjoyed being in on your news today," Maura said, smiling. Though at one time she and Callie seemed on the road to becoming fast friends, they had drifted apart as Callie found her need for companionship filled by her husband and family. Maura held no grudges; had her own family lived closer, she would spend most of her time with them. And as it was, she'd always been able to count on Doreen for support and closeness.

But that was changing. Now there was Nate.

"I'm glad you could be here today, Maura," Callie said. "Both you and Davey." She hesitated, and Maura detected a hint of uneasiness in Callie's manner. Was it the protectiveness she'd discerned earlier, as she had in Sally? Did they wonder where her loyalties lay?

"I have to thank your family for making us welcome—especially Davey." Setting her purse on the dresser next to the window, Maura thoughtfully tucked a few strands of hair into her braid. "He adores Nate, you know," she said softly. "Nate's done so much for him. He's a whole different boy than he was a few months ago, and it's because of Nate. Your brother's a fine man, Callie."

"Yes, he is." Callie perched on the wide sill behind her. "I owe you an apology, Maura," she said abruptly.

Maura glanced at her. "An apology?"

"When I came back to Iowa—" a flush crept across her cheeks "—I thought for a while that you and Drew might be...interested in each other, and it caused a lot of confusion between me and Drew."

Maura shook her head. "But why would you owe me an apology?"

Callie looked bemused. "I never knew until recently what had happened between Nate and Wayne and you. I was only about twelve or so. Oh, I heard some talk by a few of the older kids, but since Nate and my folks never mentioned it, I didn't pay much attention. It was only after I married Drew that he told me the story. And I guess I was just so embarrassed for jumping to conclusions, I felt like it came between you and me, hindered our friendship." She gave Maura a crooked smile. "And I'm sorry for that."

Maura reached out and squeezed Callie's hand. "What's past is past," she said. "Don't let it bother you a moment longer."

"Oh, I won't," Callie said with her old cheerfulness, and the two women laughed.

"Well," Maura said after a moment, "I better get on downstairs. I imagine by now I have one little boy champing at the bit."

"Or one rather large man chomping at something else," Callie teased. Behind her, Maura glimpsed the view from the window. She could see the barn, unobstructed by trees, and clear across the field behind it. Anyone standing at the window would have seen her and Nate wander off and wander back, only to disappear behind the barn for several minutes.

Maura was surprised when she didn't blush even while the memory of Nate's kisses suffused her. Whatever her face did show, it caused Callie's to soften with understanding.

"Nate is a good man," she said. "But it's always been difficult to know what he's thinking. He holds things inside. For years I never had a clue that anything had occurred between you and him. But I know now that what happened affected him, very much."

Callie looked at her with those blue-gray eyes that were so like her brother's.

"He remembers, Maura."

Here, then, was the message from the protective sister that Maura had been expecting. Though what was her point exactly? Was Callie trying to tell her what Maura already knew, that Nate had begun loving her long before the recent turn of events that had brought them together? Or was it something else, something she also already knew—that while Nate had always been reserved, the encounter with Wayne had served to magnify that tendency in him, much as Wayne's death and Davey's operation had made her son more introspective? Much as those events had made her so, as well.

Or was Callie trying to say that there was yet another unresolved matter that needed to be set to rights, made amends for, or simply acknowledged?

Was the past past?

Solemnly Maura nodded before picking up her purse to leave.

Chapter Seven

Davey had his turn on the Ferris wheel and managed to hold onto his lunch. Once his mission had been successfully executed, he felt free to sample the spoils of victory: cotton candy, corny dogs and funnel cakes. Maura winced at every bite he took and hoped Doreen had plenty of bicarbonate of soda on hand, but the cast-iron stomach that had stood him in good stead through the ride on the Ferris wheel seemed to be holding up under this additional duress.

The highlight of the afternoon was Nate's rotation at the dunking machine. Drew had set it up to benefit the local humane society: prospective dunkers paid a dollar to throw three baseballs at the bull's-eye on the end of a lever that, when hit squarely, would plunge the person sitting on the padded seat into a tank of water. It was all good, clean fun, and the proceeds went to a good cause.

Drew had recruited his friends to serve as dunkees. When Nate, Maura and Davey arrived, Hank Peterson, Maura's landlord, as well as friend to Drew and Nate, was just finishing up his turn. The gray-haired man wore an old-fashioned tank-style swimsuit and, as the crowd retired him with much applause, struck several muscle poses, much to his wife's chagrin. By the time he reached her side, where she handed him a towel, the perennially composed Cora Peterson was beet red and laughing like a girl.

"Y'old fool," she said fondly.

Nate, who'd left them to change, now appeared in a pair of cutoffs and ready for service. With a new victim at hand, the crowd cheered like Romans at the forum. Many of Nate's Little Leaguers were there, hoping to exact poetic justice by showing their coach just how well he'd taught them.

Maura stared, dry mouthed, as Nate climbed the ladder and lowered himself onto the wide board seat within the protective cage. She'd forgotten how finely built a man he was. Toes dangling in the water, he bent down, the muscles in his shoulders rippling, to scoop two handfuls of water and splash them on his browned chest. For the kids' benefit, he shivered theatrically; Maura shivered reflexively, then abruptly grew hot all over. A bead of perspiration trickled down her spine, past the bared section that Nate had pressed his palm to earlier to bring her against the rugged torso that now gleamed in the sun. Fanning herself conspicuously to dispel the sudden light-headedness that had come upon her, Maura couldn't tear her eyes from him, and so it came as no surprise when she noticed Nate looking at her, too. Even from thirty feet away, she knew his smile was all for her.

No, Maura decided then and there, she wasn't falling in love. She'd already fallen.

Davey was begging to go first, so Drew took his dollar and brought him forward in front of the normal mark. The boy took careful aim before letting his first ball fly, but it would obviously take a hard and accurate throw, even by an adult, to hit the lever just right and knock Nate off his perch. Davey looked so disappointed by his miss Nate had Drew move him forward another ten feet and told him to have another go. This one hit the lever but bounced off harmlessly. Finally Drew held Davey up within a yard of the lever. The last ball struck the bull's-eye in the middle, and Nate dropped into the tank. He came up sputtering and splashing water so that not a little of it landed on Davey and Drew. They retreated, laughing.

The rest of Davey's teammates had their turns, and Nate had his turn in the water over the next hour. Then Maura heard a murmur coming from the back of the gathering.

Kenny Foster stepped up to the mark. Pulling a crumpled dollar out of his jeans' pocket and handing it to Drew, he glanced around, obviously looking for someone. After a moment, he found Davey, who stood with Maura at the front of the crowd.

"Let me show you how it's done, sport," Kenny said with a broad wink that aroused apprehension in Maura. What was he looking to prove?

"Go to it, Kenny!" a man yelled. "He's already wet behind the ears anyway!"

Maura turned and saw Arvid Newley and his wife, Polly, a few feet away. The calls and remarks throughout the afternoon had been similarly disparaging, but Maura detected a different note in Arvid's. She knew him slightly, his wife only a little better, though Polly had attended each of Maura's gardening talks. During the entire time, the older woman had worn the same dour expression she wore now—definitely not antagonistic, but not exactly lending endorsement, either.

Kenny wound up and let the baseball fly. Like Wayne, he had excelled at this sport, but the first ball missed the lever and smacked the tarp behind it. Though Nate clapped gamely at Kenny's try, Maura could see that he'd lost the cheerful expression he'd worn since this morning.

The crowd, oblivious to the undercurrent of tension, continued to cheer Kenny on, razzing him good-naturedly when the second then third balls missed their mark. Kenny had a powerful arm, and had either of the balls landed true, Nate would have undoubtedly hit the water.

No one could mistake the grim intent in Kenny's eye as he dug three fingers into his pocket for another dollar bill. He thrust it at Drew, who seemed about to refuse it when Nate called out, "Here we go, everybody gets another chance."

Bless him, Maura thought, he was trying to be fair.

This time Kenny inhaled a deep, steadying breath before throwing the ball. It struck the lever but not square on, so while the impact jolted Nate, he remained firmly on his perch.

Kenny was all business now. He held the ball in front of him, head bent and as intent as any major-league pitcher on the mound. The throng of people around him was silent now as it became evident that this was much more than a little Fourth of July fun. Davey stood unmoving in front of Maura. She couldn't see his face, but his small body radiated with the same tension that permeated the assembly. Nate's expression now was closed, impassive as she'd ever seen it, as he waited. Maura ached for them both and wondered wildly how to stop the action, end this little showdown that Kenny seemed determined to play out. But it was all so subtle, so covert, she felt herself held immobile by the circumstances. Trapped, as Nate was trapped within the cage of chicken wire and waiting the unavoidable.

It came. The next ball hit the lever with a solid whack, and Nate plunged into the water. There was a smattering of applause, nothing like the usual roar of approval that most victors received. Maura heard Arvid's boisterous laughter carry over the muted murmurs then abruptly cut off with a wheeze not unlike air being forced out of a bagpipe. She turned to see the large man rubbing his ribs and staring after the retreating back of his wife.

"Well, Davey boy," Kenny said with a self-satisfied grin, stopping in front of the boy and Maura, "I'm all warmed up now—what say we make a run on the prizes at the baseball toss?"

Davey lifted one shoulder noncommittally and shot a quick glance toward the dunking machine. Nate was no longer in the cage, having gone to change back into his street clothes. "We were gonna go watch the ex-abition game over at the ball diamond," Davey explained. "But Gran'ma said she'd bring me back down to the carnival after supper—maybe you and me can go then."

Kenny's face was a study. If he'd expected Davey's admiration, Maura thought, he was sorely disappointed. He frowned in contemplation for only a moment before the Foster smile returned in force.

"Sure, sport," Kenny said easily. "Sounds like a plan."

He looked at her then for the first time, and having had little contact with him lately, she was again struck by his resemblance to Wayne—same build, same features, same eyes. Right now they were challenging, but something else lingered in their depths—something she'd seen in Wayne's eyes more than once.

Maura met his gaze. She understood him, understood what he was feeling, perhaps more than he understood himself right now. And she understood his fear, perhaps more than she wanted to. Her innate compassion rose up in her and ached for this man also, so like her dead husband.

But it wasn't right to split her little boy's loyalties so.

The smile faded from Kenny's face. He nodded shortly, as if to say *so that's the lay of it.* It was an acknowledgment, not a concession, for as he sauntered off, Maura knew that Kenny Foster remembered, too.

The incident at the dunking machine took a little of the shine off the day, though Nate tried to gloss over it, demonstrate that he considered it a small matter and that Maura and Davey should, too. Davey got the idea and carried on as usual, seeming to enjoy the game, but both he and Maura had drawn fractionally inward. Out of the corner of his eye, when they thought he wasn't looking, Nate saw twin worry lines mar their expressions. It brought on that restlessness

in him he'd rather not have recognized, because he knew
that for about two cents, he'd give Kenny Foster more than
a piece of his mind.

He hadn't had many dealings with Kenny over the years,
though Nate sensed that, just as with Wayne, there'd always be a wariness between him and Wayne's brother. Part
of it had to do with life in a small town. People tended to
remember slights and hold grudges far longer than was
healthy.

You oughta know, he thought ruefully. Yet he wanted less
than anything to start something with Kenny Foster. No, he
would never welcome such an encounter, one that would
only hurt Maura and Davey. But the look in Kenny's eye
made him think he couldn't avoid it forever, either.

Early evening he and Maura dropped Davey off at Doreen's before heading up to Main Street for the pig roast and
kegger. He almost suggested they spend the evening alone,
either at her house or his, but it was pure selfishness that
drove that desire; he wanted to hold her, love her, lose himself in her and ignore the rest of the world. He wanted to
avoid the Kenny Fosters and the Arvid Newleys, who in-
truded into the circle of intimacy he was so carefully con-
structing around Maura and himself. And he wanted to keep
from tarnishing any more than he already had in Maura's
eyes.

It was one of the hardest things he'd ever done, walking
with Maura up to the group of people among the scattering
of picnic tables. He knew it was not his imagination that the
chatter fell off as the crowd parted to admit them. With a
quick nod of greeting here and there, Nate steered Maura
over to where Lew Henderson, Susie's father, was taking
money.

"Hey, Maura, Nate," Lew hailed them. "I can't tell you
what a kick Susie got out of dunking her coach today."

Nate hoped Lew didn't detect his slight pause in handing
the other man a ten-dollar bill. Maura said nothing, but
Nate felt her stiffen imperceptibly.

Damn Kenny Foster, he thought with rare invective.

"Susie's got durn near the best accuracy on the team," Nate said, forcing lightness into his voice.

Lew beamed, obviously sensing nothing out of the ordinary. "She's a pistol, isn't she? Her mother's given up buying her dresses anymore. Though this morning she did sit still to get her hair curled. I do believe she's taken to your boy, uh, Maura." His gaze switched belatedly from Nate's face to Maura's, but Nate caught the slip. His stomach sank. Would Maura wonder if the whole town put him and Davey together as a unit? He knew her feelings on the matter, her fear of his taking Wayne's place in Davey's life, even taking into account the developing love between Maura and himself.

But Maura only smiled her warm, gentle smile. "She's a sweet little girl," she told Lew. "Very loyal. I don't think Davey minds having her as a special friend, either."

When they turned to get in line for the barbecue, Nate sought Maura's gaze for confirmation. His heart filled, as he knew it always would, at the sight of her generous spirit shining forth—shining for him. And he discovered then that he needn't be alone with Maura to lose himself in her.

As they got their food and drinks, Nate discovered something else—a change in the atmosphere. Both of them, but especially him, were greeted cordially as they made their way to a table, plates in hand. It was nothing obvious, just a "Hey there, Nate, how're your beans comin' up this year?" Or "Hope this good weather keeps up, don't you?" Or even a "Heard you really got those Tee-Ballers in shape this year. Hope you'll see fit to give coaching another go next year."

And the message that seeped through was that, sometime in the past few months, these people had decided to give him their support. Though word must have gotten around about what happened that afternoon, or perhaps because it had, he realized that the town was on his side, and it apparently carried over to their feelings about his farming. He could think of no other reason for the difference in attitude.

Until Hank and Cora Peterson sat down at their table.

"Well, Nathaniel," Cora said, skipping any preliminary chitchat, "I understand you're doing some pretty revolutionary things on that farm of yours."

Nate swallowed a mouthful of pork and wondered if Cora could have spoken any louder. There was an immediate lull in the conversation around them. Cora had long ago accorded herself the role of official commentator on all that happened, was about to happen or might happen in Soldier Creek. She ran the town like a major general, and the biggest reason she got away with it was because her ultimate intentions were good—although there were a few residents who said they could have lived with a little less goodness, and consequently less Cora.

Though his stomach churned, Nate calmly took another bite of his meal. Setting his elbows on the edge of the table, he grasped one fist in the palm of his other hand and met Cora's bespectacled gaze unblinkingly. "I'm implementing a few progressive techniques I've been reading about for some time, if that's what you mean by 'revolutionary,' Cora."

"Yes, but what about this biodiversifying and wetlands restoration, and how you're looking to take care of the environment? Maura's been telling all the ladies in town about it, you know."

He didn't know. For once completely astonished out of his reticence, Nate whipped his gaze to Maura, who sat next to him. Her own gaze was downcast as she studied her hands, clasped in her lap. For one insane moment, he wondered if she were embarrassed to be linked so publicly to Crazy Nate and his crazy ways. Then a glorious blush rose from her neckline and stole upward into her cheeks, making her glow. It was the kind of glow, Nate thought, that a woman gets when she's been discovered...when she's in love.

It took every ounce of his strength not to pull her into his arms and kiss the stuffing out of her then and there. He settled for slipping his hand into hers under the table. Her fingers twined with his and squeezed.

When he finally looked away from her, he found both Hank and Cora waiting with innocent interest. "I, uh, I don't mind talking to you about my work, Cora, if you're interested."

"Oh, I *am*," Cora pronounced definitely. "In this day and age, how could anyone *not* be interested in preserving our precious resources? The ladies have agreed you can't continue to keep all that information to yourself. It's just fascinating...simply fascinating."

Nate wasn't so obtuse he didn't realize what Cora was doing. He permitted himself a quick scan of the surrounding tables. There was still a measure of skepticism in people's faces—wouldn't be Iowa without it—but he found something else, too: tolerance, acknowledgment of his effort if not all-out approval. He hadn't asked for acceptance, by any means, but he realized he now had it—through Maura. And it felt good.

His inspection was arrested by a pair of eyes just over Cora's shoulder. Sitting next to Arvid, who was oblivious to his surroundings as he devoured a heaping plate of barbecue, was Polly Newley. The extremes in Iowa's weather took their toll on some people more than others; Polly couldn't have been more than midfifties, yet she looked ten years older. Her lips pinched together, she scrutinized Nate with faded blue eyes. Then, so subtly he wondered if he imagined it, Polly nodded once.

Drew and Callie arrived, and the evening of good food and conversation progressed. A section of the street had been roped off for dancing, and at dusk the disk jockey started spinning tunes. Nate was dying to get Maura out on the dance floor for a few moments of relative privacy, but he wanted to wait for just the right song.

It soon arrived. With Bonnie Raitt singing sassily about giving people "Something to Talk About," he took Maura's hand and steered her to one of the less crowded corners of the dance area. He tucked her against him and gave her a devilish grin when she raised her brows at his selection.

"I didn't know you were such a good dancer, Nate Farrell," she said after a moment.

"No?" He executed a turn that made her grip his shoulder and brought her more snugly into his embrace. "Well, Maura Foster, I've got talents you've never even dreamed of, if I do say so myself."

Never would he tire of those shy brown eyes and that incredible rosiness! He felt as if he were making friends with a fawn—a delicate process of coaxing and clucking reassurances as he held an irresistible tidbit just out of reach and watched while she responded with demure caution, drawn to him in spite of herself.... She was right, there was a certain power in it.... *Come closer, sweet, I promise I won't hurt you. I'd never hurt you.*

"I didn't know," he said abruptly.

"Know what?"

"That you were spending your evenings talking about my farming to a bunch of women who couldn't be any more receptive than their husbands."

"Well, I didn't ask them to adopt your theories," she explained. "I merely made certain points by using you as an example."

"Is that all?"

"No... I thought they should also accept your right to farm as you saw fit," she answered with a defensive lift of her chin, as if he would scold her for her efforts.

Scolding was the furthest thing from his mind. "And in your own way, you brought them to understanding."

"I don't know if they understand any better than they did before, but I do think that the winds of change, they are a-blowing."

"I think so, too." Nate bent his head, pressing his cheek against her temple. "Thank you, Maura," he whispered, "for sticking up for me."

Her breath warm against his neck, she answered, "You're welcome, Nate."

On top of the world, he wanted to tell her how much he loved her, but not here. This wasn't the place or the time. Soon, though...

"I don't know about you guys," a voice broke into his thoughts, "but somethin' puts me in the mind to hear Patsy Cline singin' 'Crazy.'"

Nate turned, Maura still in his arms. Kenny Foster stood a few feet away, thumb hooked in a belt loop, a plastic cup of beer in his other hand. On either side of him stood a few of his friends, twenty-four- or -five-year-olds like Kenny. They snickered at his remark.

Kenny's eyes were bright, Nate noticed. Too bright. He'd had a few beers—not enough he wouldn't realize what he was doing, but plenty enough to give him the nerve to do it.

Durn and tarnation. The scene was a replay of that day at Ernie's, evoking in Nate all the same reactions. *It's better to just walk away.* At least this time Davey wasn't here—although he was probably the only person in town who wasn't.

"If there's something you want to hear," Nate said, "I'm sure the DJ is taking requests."

"Yeah? Well, I got somethin' for you, Farrell, and it isn't a request."

There was a startled murmur from the crowd. Nate dropped the arm that held Maura and unobtrusively adjusted his stance so she was behind him. Out of the corner of his eye, he saw Drew and even Hank saunter closer, as if without design. He was thankful for their presence—not that he thought there'd be a fight. At least he hoped there wouldn't be, for Maura's sake.

"Time to call it a night, don't you think, Kenny?" he tried again, hoping to snuff the challenge flickering in Kenny's eyes.

"Might be time to call it somethin' else, if you ask me, Farrell," the young man said. "Can't you tell when you're not wanted somewhere?" He locked his jaw belligerently. No, Nate judged, the kid was set on starting a brawl.

Then Nate saw it, and for an instant he was thirteen years in the past, standing on Maura's porch. He saw not Kenny Foster but his brother Wayne, with the same, almost insensible fear in the depth of his eyes.

This wasn't Wayne, though; it was Kenny. And his fear wasn't one of losing Maura. It was a fear of losing Wayne. Nate ought to recognize that fear—he'd seen the same apprehension in Maura's eyes more than he wanted to.

And this confrontation wasn't even personal, Nate realized. It certainly wasn't about his farming. To Kenny, Nate represented the final confirmation of Wayne Foster's death.

I'm sorry, Nate wanted to tell him, tell Maura, too. *I'm truly sorry, but Wayne is gone. You're here, Maura, and I don't plan to lose you again.* He understood, but this heartache had to end, for all of them.

That resolve must have shown on his face, for Kenny took a threatening step forward, hands clenched at his sides. Nate tensed in readiness, moving away from Maura. She clung to his arm.

"Please, Nate," she begged in a whisper, close to his shoulder.

Nate spared a quick glance away from Kenny. Maura stared up at him. Her face was stark with disbelief that this was happening—again. *Not here, not now,* she seemed to say. She knew as well as he that no good would come out of a public confrontation.

But what choice did he have? "What would you have me do, Maura?" he asked in a low voice. "He's the one spoiling for a fight, thinking it'll prove something."

"Please, Nate."

"Don't ask me to back down again." He would have died for her, but this was something she couldn't ask him to do.

She swung around to her brother-in-law. "Kenny." The appeal in her gaze seemed almost frantic.

Suddenly Nate knew what he wanted, what critical need within himself cried to be met: he needed Maura to choose... to choose *him,* as she hadn't those years ago. He wouldn't have done it this way, but now that the moment was here, he had to know that she would pick him over Kenny and what the other man represented in her life.

Nate remained set. He waited, as everyone did, including Kenny, for the next move. It would have to be Maura's. There was just no other way.

Maura must have realized it, too. Every emotion in the spectrum crossed her expressive face: anger and frustration, compassion and despair. Her gaze jumped back and forth between the two men. Finally she dropped her chin, turned and walked away, the crowd parting for her.

She would not choose.

Kenny watched her retreat before meeting Nate's eyes. A gratified smile lurked on his lips, one that Nate would have taken great pleasure in wiping off his face. He knew as well as Nate that what had been settled tonight was that nothing was settled.

That sensation of boiling, restless energy, powerful and dangerous, built in Nate, making him feel he would explode if he did not find a release valve for it. He had to get out of there, fast.

He turned to follow Maura.

Nate found her in her garden, as he'd known he would. Silently he stood just beyond the brick edging and watched her. She knelt between the rows, soiling her pretty dress, but she didn't seem to notice as she plucked and tucked the plants here and there. He would have loved to seek the same solace, that comfort both of them found in the land, but he knew walking away from her now would cause something to die between them. They had to work this out.

"Maura."

No answer.

"Come into the house, Maura."

"Why?" She didn't look up.

"Because we need to talk, and durn if I'll do it out here where half the county can hear us."

He half suspected she'd argue, or at least flash him one of those defiant glares, but Maura rose smoothly, brushing off her dress. With an unapproachable expression on her face that reminded him of Davey, she walked right past him without a glance, across the yard and up the back-porch steps. The screen door shut with deceptive calm.

Inside he found her washing up at the kitchen sink. It was when he saw her hands trembling as she dried them that he realized that she *was* angry, incredibly angry. His gentle Maura. And he perceived how angry he was, too. Angry that another Foster had come between them.

"I'm sorry for that whole scene," he finally said. "Sorry it had to come to that." His jaw tensed. He wanted to explain or justify, but the right words weren't coming to him. "Kenny had no call to do what he did this afternoon or just now," he declared.

"Neither did you!" she shot back, looking at him fully now, her face flushed with indignation. "Nate, how could you?"

"How could I do what?" he asked in disbelief.

"How could you do that to me, stand there and practically challenge me to pick one of you over the other?"

"Wait a minute." He ran his hand through his hair, trying to maintain his composure. "I'm not looking to prove anything to Kenny Foster or anyone else, but if he's going to draw lines and dare me to step over 'em, then by God, Maura, I will."

"Go ahead, then." She waved a dismissing hand at him. "Go on back uptown and have it out with him. And then tell me what you *do* prove. That one of you is stronger than the other? That, because you can lick him, then you win me or Davey, like a prize at the carnival?''

"If that's the only kind of logic Kenny can understand, then yes!'' he exploded. He blew out a lungful of air and gripped the back of a nearby chair with one hand. "I don't know why I'm the one at fault here.''

"You're not. No one is, but...'' She sank her teeth into her bottom lip, obviously as confused as he was and as frustrated by that confusion. "Kenny's afraid, Nate!'' she said. "I'm not saying his actions are honorable or right or logical, but he's afraid. How can I just flat out reject him and his concerns when he's feeling nothing I haven't felt myself? Even if he is the one who pushed the issue!'' She shook her head. "I don't know what I wanted to happen. All I knew was that he wasn't rational, and you were. And I thought you understood, Nate.''

"I do understand! But won't you understand *me*, Maura? I backed off once because I thought that was what you wanted, but I'm here to tell you I won't do it again. I won't lose you. I can't lose you, because I love you.''

It wasn't how he would have had it come out, and he knew he wasn't saying something they both didn't know. Yet such words would always count more than others. At their uttering, he saw Maura's expression soften and then, alarmingly, crumple in absolute misery. She turned away, her face in her hands. Clearly this wasn't what she wanted to hear.

Nate was stunned. God, had he been wrong to think he'd seen love in her eyes, that her actions—standing up for him to the townspeople—spoke of her regard for him as surely as if she'd told him so?

They stood in silence for indeterminable minutes. Finally it was Maura who spoke first. "You once said, Nate, that maybe it was me who'd changed in the past two years. Not the rest of the world. And you were right—I *have* changed. A person has to change when their life's torn in two.''

She raised her head. In profile, her features were calm though drawn in pain. "What a shock it was—one day I was going about my business, married to Wayne, raising our son. The next day I was burying my husband. I don't know how I could have saved the piece of me that died with him. Faith or hope or whatever you want to call it. But after two years, I thought I'd found... peace. I was proud that I'd adjusted. Maybe not the best way, but the best I knew how.

"And then you came along, showed me... Oh, you showed me a lot of things. Mostly that I might've made—" her voice dropped to a whisper "—that there might have been a better choice years ago. I don't regret marrying Wayne and I could never, ever regret Davey. But now I'm finding out there's more to faith and hope and love than... what I had with Wayne." She clenched her hand against her chest. "I missed something very vital because I was forced into a decision once. I won't make the same mistake again."

She looked at him, and the mettle he'd glimpsed before in this very kitchen shone from her eyes. "I love you, too, Nate. But I won't live my life that way, not anymore. I can't do it. It's not right."

A deep ache had started in him at her words. He knew now what she feared most: having no choice, no control over the events that had changed and would change her life. He also knew that, yes, she loved him, but somehow he'd failed, by both word and deed, to bring her the happiness she so wanted and deserved.

Yet he knew he couldn't have acted differently and been able to live with himself.

How could it be that a man and a woman, two people truly in love, could not find accord? *This* wasn't right. It went against the laws of nature, against the faith on which he'd built his own life, and it set upon him a fear not unlike Maura's. For even in nature, aberrations occurred. Even now, now that they loved each other, the impossible could happen. He *could* lose her.

Nate felt himself withdraw from her as surely as if he'd turned and walked out of her house. *Leave,* an inner voice urged him. *It's better to walk away, especially if staying won't solve anything.*

Yet he remained, locked into place by his love for this woman, even though there seemed nothing he could say, nothing he could do to change the past and nothing to sell her on the future except the love between them. "Maura, I—" he began, then cut himself off. Never had he felt so inarticulate, at a loss for the words he'd never put much stock into. But he had to try. "I'm not asking that some big life-or-death decision be made here tonight. This whole business with Kenny, it's taken both of us by surprise. Neither of us expected to be put on the spot like that. Why don't we just do what we have been—take it one day at a time."

She nodded, her expression remote as she also drew inward to regroup, as if after a battle. She stood a few feet away from him in the darkened kitchen, her arms wrapped around her middle in the manner that Davey had hugged himself when his own small world had been set on end.

Yes, there was Davey to think about, too. Nate hoped Kenny wouldn't confront Maura again, but if he did, Kenny had a powerful bargaining chip in Wayne's son. Nate knew how she felt about maintaining the link between Davey and his father, the tie by blood.

Yet there was no substitute for love, and Nate loved that little boy as if he were his own. He would do anything to preserve Davey's happiness—and Maura's.

Even if it meant walking out of their lives?

That sense of churning energy barely held in check surged within him, stronger than ever. A little break from people in general might not be a bad idea. He had a notion that were he to come face-to-face with Kenny Foster any time in the next month, he'd not be able to temper his actions.

"I promised Davey I'd take him out to Callie and Drew's place to see the horses tomorrow," he said stiffly. "I'd like to keep the commitment."

Her startled gaze flew to his. "Of course, Nate. I wouldn't dream of not letting you see him any more than I would Doreen. Or Kenny," she added, not as an afterthought, but in emphasis.

He hesitated again, feeling it was like yanking out a primary organ for him to speak, but he had to say one more thing, more for himself than her. "Believe me, Maura, I know you've got some considerations to take into account, with Davey and Doreen and Kenny. I respect those concerns, but I want you to know it'll take more than the three of them to keep us apart for long."

That said, he clamped down on his molars and pivoted toward the door, not wanting to see it if she got that challenging spark in her eyes that set him off every time. Not wanting her to see the doubt in his own eyes that belied his words.

But he stopped at the door. He didn't want to leave like this, not after experiencing the closeness that had sprung up between them so quickly, so surely.

"Nate—"

He turned. Her eyes held an appeal. Relief washed over him as he saw that she, too, regretted this turn of events. It made him feel that somehow they'd find a solution to this situation.

He held out his hand, palm down, and she stepped forward and took it. Nate hesitated, then bent his head as she lifted her chin. Softly their lips met.

He hadn't thought the kiss would be much more than a gesture of reconciliation, but Maura parted her lips instantly under his. Without thinking, he nudged her mouth open wider still, sinking into the familiar and yet still so new taste of her.

He pulled her around to face him and into the circle of his arms. She pressed close, palms resting on his chest, and he felt his skin grow hot as a brand under her touch. Nate fought to control himself as he had with her from the beginning, but her small, urging moan finally broke his restraint. He crushed her to him as the floodgates burst, and he poured himself into her as the restlessness in him found its release at last.

One arm surrounded her shoulders, the hand of the other clamped like a vise to the back of her head as he guided his onslaught of her responsive mouth. His fingers dug into her hair and became tangled in the constricting braid. With a groan of sheer frustration, he closed his fingers over it and slid down its length to the bow at the end. With a tug that brought her head farther back, exposing the vulnerable expanse of her neck to him, he pulled the bow and the covered band beneath it from her hair.

Impatiently, his lips finding the racing pulse at her throat, Nate unplaited the braid and spread the silky strands. They were cool and incredibly soft between his fingers. And he realized that he hadn't even known how much he'd wanted to feel her hair loose in his hands.

He felt cheated—of the anticipation, of the discovery that shouldn't have come as a shock but in the manner that two people should learn about one another: slowly, leisurely, with a tenderness that was a discovery in itself. Suddenly he wanted back that moment when he'd stood with Maura on her front porch, knowing that her teenage heart had never experienced romantic love or its physical expression.

What he wanted was to be her first. And he would never, ever be her first.

The thought spurred him to pull her closer as if in an effort to obliterate the fact from both their minds. Maura clung to him nearly as urgently, her hands spreading across his back, clutching him desperately.

There definitely was a power here. At that moment, he knew he could have taken her into her prim bedroom, all done up in green and white like a schoolgirl's, and made her truly his. She wouldn't resist him; she wanted it as much as he did, this losing of self in another, annihilating all doubts. How he wanted her, to show her what they could feel together! He knew he could, too. She had admitted she'd never known the kind of passion that sprang up between them so quickly.

Abruptly Nate's heart eased. And he realized he'd been given a gift, the one he'd wanted most: he *was* her first, the most important of all—though not the first to lie with her and give her a child. Still, it satisfied him soul deep to know he was the first to whom she'd given all of her heart.

This was his bargaining chip. But he didn't want to use it to cast a spell over her. She must come to him of her own rational volition. She must have the chance to choose.

He lifted his head and pressed her cheek against his shoulder as he stroked his hand through her hair, his heart pounding like a jackhammer. "I'd better go," he whispered, voice rough with the desire he was slowly bringing back to rein.

Her arms tightened about him briefly, a small protest that told him she had yet to regain her equilibrium, as well.

"Yes," she answered softly after a moment.

He gave her a squeeze before letting her go. "Tell Davey I'll be by around ten."

"All right." With her eyes downcast, her lips glistening and swollen from his kisses and her golden hair in a riot around her face, she looked like a reluctant angel. Or a fallen one. Fallen at his hand. The thought threw him into an even greater state of disruption.

This time he made it out the door and to his pickup. Jerking the stick shift into gear, he spun out of Maura's driveway as the urgency grew ever more intense. Within seconds he was on the road out of town; in only minutes more he pulled into his own drive. With wide strides, he crossed the expanse of lawn, away from the house.

And beneath the eye of a full moon, Nate walked his fields until dawn.

Chapter Eight

Maura knocked at Doreen's back door the next morning. She heard the pounding of rubber-soled feet that were definitely not her mother-in-law's.

"Hi, Mom." Davey peered up at her through the screen. "Gran'ma said I could watch cartoons while I eat breakfast," he explained right off the bat, likely because such amenities weren't permitted at their house.

"He's being real careful," Doreen added as Maura stepped inside the house and Davey raced back to his morning treat. The older woman sat at the kitchen table reading the newspaper. She nodded toward the coffeepot. "Pour a cup and have a chair," she invited.

Maura hesitated. She'd hoped to collect Davey and leave, but she realized she should have expected to stay and chat awhile. "That sounds good," she said.

"I was going to send Davey home with his things in a half hour or so," Doreen continued as Maura took a cup from the rack on the counter. "Didn't mean for you to interrupt your day."

"Yes, well," Maura said lightly, her back to the other woman, "I woke up rather early this morning and got all my chores out of the way. The walk over seemed like a nice break." Hopefully Doreen would accept that brief explanation of the circles under Maura's eyes, which spoke more of a sleepless night than an early morning.

Because it had been a sleepless night. Entirely. After tossing in her bed for four hours, she'd finally risen and dressed. Unable to abide the picture she'd have made poking around and muttering in her garden at 3:00 a.m., she confined herself to the house. She repotted five plants, rooted the cuttings from others and started half a dozen new cuttings. She pruned and fertilized and found not one moment of peace in the occupation that had always been her single guaranteed escape from her problems.

But she still felt she was drowning, that nowhere could she set down a foot and secure herself. And regain control. In her mind's eye, when she thought of Kenny, she saw Wayne...Wayne, smiling and cheerful, everybody's friend...Wayne, desperate to hold on to her at all costs.

Pulling out a chair, Maura sat down with her coffee and tried to redirect the thoughts that surely showed on her face. Under cover of scratching her forehead, she felt for and found the ridge of flesh between her brows that Nate had pinpointed as proclaiming her state of mind. Maura tried to smooth it away with her fingertips.

She glanced up to find Doreen's concerned gaze on her. "Are you all right, dear?" she asked.

Suddenly Maura knew why she'd come. Far from hiding her worries, she *wanted* to talk to Doreen—about Kenny and Davey and Wayne and Doreen herself. Someone who knew what she was going through. But how to begin? And how could she dredge up memories painful to Doreen, ones that Maura had hoped were finally put well behind them all?

How could she tell this woman of the anger she felt toward both her sons? Anger that one of them had died, anger that the other would not let him remain dead.

Maura wrapped her hands around her coffee cup to keep them from shaking as she tried to master the emotions that surfaced so quickly these days—ever since Nate had found them as they lay buried within the bedrock of her dormant heart.

Nate. He was why she was here, too. Through all her tossing and turning and agonizing last night, which had only left her mind in more of a muddle, one thing had remained crystal clear: she loved Nate. That fact was her anchor in all of this turmoil.

"I don't know if you've heard about it or not, Doreen," she said, "but there was a bit of a scene at the dance last night."

Doreen nodded. "Yesterday afternoon, too, I understand from Cora Peterson."

"Cora actually called you?" Maura asked in astonishment, thinking someone ought to put a muzzle on the woman.

"I believe her intent was charitable," Doreen said with a chuckle at Maura's tone. "Both she and Hank are pretty fond of you and Davey."

She rose and poured herself another cup of coffee. "You know, I've never gotten to know Cora very well. Thought it best to just stay out of her way, especially when she was set on getting it. But I have to admit I wished I'd been a little more like her when she snatched up the most marriageable bachelor in town—I mean, the one a woman my age might have had a chance at."

She resumed her seat as Maura stared at her. "You...you had your eye on Hank Peterson?" she stammered.

"Oh, I wouldn't put it so plain as that." Doreen took a sip of her coffee and actually blushed. "I thought he was a fine-looking man, so nice and friendly when he came into the co-op for one thing or another. Always stopped to say hello and chat a minute with me. But, you know, life in this town moves kind of slow. Gives everybody a chance to examine it pretty closely as it goes on by. I didn't want people to talk about Morley Foster's lonely old widow being on a man-hunt." She folded the newspaper in front of her and set it aside. "To tell the truth, though, the real reason is I wasn't sure I was up to thinking about having another man in Morley's house, and I didn't know if I wanted to put a good man through having to think about it, either."

Doreen lifted her shoulders. "So I didn't do anything except go on having nice chats with Hank Peterson, figuring if something was meant to happen, it would. And it did— here I sit in Morley's house, getting lonelier and older while Cora Peterson's got Hank in hers."

Tears sprang to Maura's eyes as she reached for Doreen's hand. "I...I didn't know, Doreen. I mean, I knew you missed Morley very much, but I didn't think... You'll always have me and Davey, you know that, don't you?"

"Yes, I do," Doreen said, patting Maura's hand reassuringly. "I'm just sorry Kenny doesn't realize that. Lord, he's like Wayne. Wears his feelings right out there on his sleeve in a way that puts a burden on those who love him. Just about the opposite of Davey. And you."

She sighed, her gaze focused inward as she continued. "I worry about Kenny. He's never had to get over Wayne's death, or Morley's, either, for that matter. He's been out on the road since he graduated high school, and when he's in town, he's driving into Newton with his friends. He hasn't had to deal with waking up to a quiet house that once upon a time was never quiet. Never had to remember to peel one potato instead of two or three or four. He's never gotten used to sharing life's daily burdens, so that now he hates every reminder he's got to shoulder them all by himself."

Doreen looked at Maura, her eyes filled with the same sympathy Maura had felt for the older woman moments before. "Kenny's got some things to work out, Maura, and I'm afraid he's going to grab at any finger hold he can on the way to stop the process. If it was me he was holding on to, I'd try to reason with him myself. But it's you and Davey he's fixed on. It's going to have to come from you. I don't know what advice to give you to deal with him. All I ask is that you forgive him for putting you through this, and forgive yourself for having to put him through it."

A tear sped down Maura's cheek as she gripped the older woman's fingers in silent assent—and thanks. Yes, Doreen did understand completely. Suddenly she regretted that she hadn't talked to her mother-in-law more over the past two years of her feelings about Wayne's death. Truly her reasons had been that she hadn't wanted to add to the older woman's suffering with her own. But Maura knew now that Doreen accepted the fact that change, both good and bad, was inevitable, and that to resist change was to remain stagnant, never giving yourself the chance to branch out and grow.

Neither was happiness static. You had to actively pursue it, even if it meant taking a few risks along the way—as Nate had with his farming. Even if it meant leaving behind some security, as Davey had with her. Even if it meant letting go of memories, as she must with Wayne. Fate had seen fit to give both her and Nate another chance to discover each other. She'd be a fool not to grasp it with both hands.

"Well," Doreen said briskly, breaking into her thoughts. She gave a telltale sniff. "What have you and Davey got planned for the rest of the holiday weekend?"

"Nate's taking Davey out to see Callie and Drew's horses," Maura answered.

"Davey should love that." Doreen stacked Maura's empty cup in her own and took them to the sink. "You know, he's really changed in the last few months. He's happier."

Maura moved beside her as she laid a spoon next to the cups. "Yes, with Little League and getting rid of his glasses, he's hardly the same boy he used to be."

"I'm sure those things are part of the reason. But most of it's because you're happier, too, Maura. And it's more than your getting into your own house and working at a good job."

Maura nodded. "I know," she said softly.

Doreen slid an arm around her shoulders. "It's good to see you both enjoying life again. It's good to see you happy."

They stood together like that for a few minutes, staring out the window over the sink.

"You know," Doreen said, "I ought to give Callie or her mother a call about how a person goes about setting up a bed-and-breakfast inn."

"You mean here?" Maura asked in surprise.

"Sure. I don't have the means to do anything fancy, and I wouldn't want more work than I could handle. But it might be fun to cook for more than just me again, or meet some interesting people."

"Like some nice, friendly man with a minute or two to chat?" Maura asked with a gentle smile.

"I can't say as I'd mind," Doreen said with a smile of her own as she went to fetch her grandson.

Nate picked up Davey at ten on the dot, coming to the house for the boy. Maura met him at the door, trying not to look too closely at him for fear of reading too much or too little in his eyes. But his gaze devoured her, locked her to him, and she saw that he'd had a rough night, as well.

"Hi, Nate." Davey's greeting was markedly subdued, compared to his ebullient welcome only twenty-four hours before.

"Hey, pard," Nate said, his eyes still on her. "We have to talk," he told her briefly in an exact echo of her thoughts, his hand resting gently on Davey's head in a statement of reassurance. Yesterday, she knew, had had its effect on Davey. Whatever happened, Nate seemed to be telling her son—and her—he would always be there for the boy.

Impossibly her heart filled with even more love for this man. She wanted to give him her own reassurances, take him in her arms and soothe away his worries as she would Davey's.

It'll be all right. Trust me.

She gave them both a smile she hoped conveyed her thoughts. "I'll have lunch waiting when you get back."

Two hours later, Maura heard a vehicle pull up just as she finished setting the small table in her kitchen. She felt a rush of anticipation that turned to dismay as soon as she glanced out the window and saw Kenny getting out of his truck.

Her first thought was for Nate. She wouldn't let Kenny involve Nate in a matter that was between her and her brother-in-law. Not again. But Nate and Davey were due back any minute.

Calmly, she went to the door. "Hello, Kenny."

"Maura," he said with a nod. His eyes rested on her speculatively for an instant before sliding away, as if he wanted to avoid whatever message might be in her gaze. "Can I come in?"

"For just a moment."

He stepped inside, glancing around her living room. "You've got a nice place here," he remarked. He, too, seemed subdued, with all the brash cockiness of yesterday gone. "Sorry I haven't been over to see it since you moved, but I'm on the road a lot." He tried for an apologetic grin. "I guess that's no excuse not to look in on my brother's family."

She said nothing, waiting.

"Is Davey here?"

"He and Nate are due back soon for lunch." Not an explanation, just fact.

A flash of irritation swept over his features before he schooled them. "I, uh, I wanted to let you know I'm sorry about the way I acted last night. Part of it must've been the beer talkin'." He grimaced and hung his head, a blond shock of hair flopping onto his forehead. "No, it was me, all the way. I don't know what to tell you, Maura. Why it rankled me to see you and . . . Nate Farrell together. I guess it just came as a surprise, finding out all at once that you and him were seeing each other. I wasn't looking for it, and it was a shocker."

"I understood that, Kenny," Maura said softly. He looked so contrite she wondered if perhaps Doreen had blown the situation with Kenny out of proportion. Perhaps they all had. She wouldn't have thought so last night, but now he seemed to realize how unreasonable and unfair his actions were.

"You weren't the only one in town, I imagine, who was surprised," she conceded. "That was our first time out as a couple."

"Really?" His head came up. "I heard he's been coaching Davey in Little League, spending a lot of time with him."

"He has, and they're very fond of each other. But that's Davey and Nate, not Nate and me."

Kenny returned her steady look with one of his own. Then he broke eye contact, letting his gaze wander around the room before settling on her again.

"Would you marry me, Maura?" he blurted out.

He couldn't have surprised her more had he announced he'd given up baseball for knitting. *"What?"*

At her clearly incredulous tone, his mouth slanted into that belligerent angle that made him look like Davey, and just about as young. "If you're looking around for a husband, why not me?"

"Don't be ridiculous!"

"Why is it so ridiculous? I know I haven't been around much, but I can find another job where I won't have to travel. I don't know what I'd do, but you can be certain it'll be more secure than this gamble Crazy Nate's taking with his land. And if I were around more, you'd see how I could take care of things for you, too. I could be the one to take Davey to Little League. I'm his uncle—and who'd be a better father for Davey than his own uncle?"

Maura opened her mouth to argue, but nothing came out. How did one refute an irrational proposition? Her head spun with the absurdity of it. Then came the anger, even more fierce than it had been last night. "You're the one who's acting crazy," she said. "I don't love you, Kenny. I couldn't love you, not that way."

"That's my point! How do you know you couldn't? I'm a lot like Wayne, and you loved him."

"Yes, but—"

"So why would marrying me be such a crazy notion?"

"Because it's not simply a matter of my 'looking for a husband'!"

"Fine, but can you tell me Nate Farrell's not looking for a wife?"

She made a sound of disbelief. "Say he is—did you actually hope that by asking me to marry you before he might, you'd get first dibs?"

"I hoped you'd give a thought to your future and Davey's!" he stormed.

Maura felt all the anger go right out of her. "Don't you know that's all I've thought about for two years? How we would survive? What either of us had to look forward to? Where we could even find the courage to look forward, knowing what the past had left behind?"

Sorrowfully she looked up at this young man, so like Wayne. "Is that what you're offering, Kenny, what you think I need? Because I'm not looking for security or guarantees. You can't give them to me any more than Nate can. That's not why I care for him."

"The only reason you're seeing him is because he's convenient," Kenny protested wildly. "He's always favored you, and now that my brother's gone, there's nothing to stop him from moving in to take Wayne's place!"

"That's right, Kenny." She grasped his upper arms in emphasis of her words. "Wayne's gone. I know it's hard to accept that there's nothing anyone can do to bring him back. But I hope we—you and I and Davey and Doreen—can find comfort in the fact that there's no one who can take his place. That includes you."

He averted his face in denial. Maura took a deep breath, knowing she had to put it to him in no uncertain terms, or he would never confront his pain and heal. "Kenny, listen to me. Davey will always be Wayne's son. Nothing can change that. But he deserves to be happy. Don't you think Wayne would want him to be happy?"

"Yes, but—"

"No, Kenny," she interrupted. "There're no 'buts' about it. I know that's what Wayne would want for both of us, however we can find that happiness."

"You mean Nate Farrell," he mumbled sullenly.

"I do. I love him, Kenny. I mean to be his wife, if he'll have me."

As soon as the words left her mouth, Maura experienced a powerful sense of completion. This was what she wanted: to love Nate without the restrictions of the past. To look forward to a future with him without guilt or fear.

Kenny closed his eyes, resistance in every fiber of him. "And if Nate won't have you?" he asked in a low voice.

Maura's fingers tightened on his arms. "Don't you dare pull another stunt like—"

She was interrupted by the whine of disk brakes outside. Both of them turned and watched through the large front window as Nate got out of his pickup. A blond head bobbed down on the other side and traveled around to the front of the truck. Davey came abruptly to a halt, as Nate had, at the sight of his mother and uncle visible through the window, obviously locked in debate.

Kenny shook off her hold on him and was out the door before she had a chance to stop him. He charged down the steps and came to a standstill in the middle of the yard as Nate took the half-dozen steps forward to meet him there. Maura made it out to the porch, but her flight to follow Kenny was arrested by Nate's face.

His expression was as remote as she'd ever seen it, carved in stone, his blue-gray eyes ice. His stance was set wide, primed for any movement on Kenny's part. He looked dangerous; he looked ready and willing to defend his very life.

Clearly Nate would stand his ground, but he was hurting, too, drawing inward for protection.

She felt the most unholy fear she had ever experienced, and knew why. Last night, she'd told Nate she wouldn't be given an ultimatum. So now, if Kenny provoked one, Nate would see himself in an impossible situation—because if he rose to the challenge, he believed he'd alienate her and lose her.

But if he were made to back down again, Maura knew it would be the last time he'd do so. And she'd lose him, this time forever.

She felt rooted in her powerlessness. Kenny was on a hair trigger, ready to go off at a second's notice. There was no reasoning with him, no stopping some kind of confrontation. Tension radiated from both men, but in Nate it took shape in that overwhelming intensity. How she'd often seen it before in his eyes, witnessed it in his commitments. Felt it in his kisses. Once that intensity had frightened her, but no more. She wanted it, needed it as much as she needed air to live.

I won't let this happen, Maura thought with clear resolution. *I won't lose Nate.*

"Kenny, Nate," she said quietly, approaching them slowly, as she would wild animals. "Let's wait a moment and—"

"Take Davey inside, Maura," Nate interrupted, his eyes never leaving Kenny.

Her gaze flew to her son. She'd actually forgotten he stood there, next to Nate's pickup.

He shook his head vehemently at Nate's command. "Uh-uh!" he said, his face drawn with apprehension, his eyes filled with the same dread she knew hers were as he watched the two men he loved most squaring off.

"Davey!" She ran to him. *Please spare my son this ordeal if nothing else,* she prayed, catching Davey's hand to take him inside as quickly as possible so she could return to try to keep this decisive conflict from even starting.

He fought her grasp, though. "I ain't leavin'!" he cried, digging in his heels.

"Davey, please." She managed to drag him halfway to the house before he broke her hold on him. He didn't run, though. He just stood there in front of her, his small chest heaving as his eyes pleaded with her not to decide his fate without him.

"Dave."

He turned to Nate.

Blue-gray eyes met brown and asked for trust. "Go on, son," he said gently.

Davey's chin quivered as it dropped. He stared at the ground a moment, clearly on the verge of disobeying. Then he whirled and ran to the house.

Maura watched him go inside before turning back to Nate and Kenny. "Surely you can see this can't go any further," she insisted. "For Davey's sake, if no one else's."

"That's right," Kenny agreed, casting a baleful eye at Nate. Clearly the exchange between Nate and Davey, illustrating their closeness, goaded Kenny. "He's my brother's son, and I've got a responsibility to look after his welfare."

"That's not what I meant!" Maura exclaimed, appalled that she'd just handed Kenny the very ammunition he needed.

"It's true, though," Kenny said. "I don't know where you find the nerve to come around here in the first place. Crazy Nate," he jeered. "Takin' chances with your own livelihood is your own damn business, but you've got no call to involve Maura or Davey in some fool undertaking that'll probably bankrupt you and ruin your land for anyone else to use."

"Kenny, stop it right now!" Maura demanded.

He didn't even acknowledge she'd spoken. With unbelievable foolhardiness, Kenny went on without drawing a breath. His color was high, his voice driven with fear.

A chill bolted down Maura's spine. She could have been looking at Wayne.

"I don't know how you can do it, Farrell, use that fatherless little kid, worm your way into his affections just so's you can get close to his mother. You don't care about either of 'em—you've just never been able to stomach losing Maura to my brother!"

It was the last straw. An ominous spark leapt into Nate's eyes, and she knew it'd take little else for him to deck Kenny. She wouldn't blame him—she'd have done it herself had she the strength. And she knew that regardless of Kenny's feelings or hers or even Davey's, she had to step forward and stick up for Nate, once and for all.

She opened her mouth to speak, but something in Nate's face stopped her. He didn't move a muscle, but she realized he would not only be unwelcoming of her interference right now, but he would also never forgive her for it.

"You're right about one thing," he said to Kenny. "It is my own damn business what I do. And it's Maura's business what she does. You want to rail on me, Foster, go right ahead. Call me names, tell me I'm not worth the dirt I plant corn in. Even prove it if you can. I won't fight you. But it all comes down to one thing—Maura's life is still her own. She's got a right to live it as she sees fit, without you, me or anybody else telling her how to do it. And by God, that's something I will fight for."

Thick tears gathered in Maura's throat as she stood there and heard Nate Farrell, never a man easy with words, express as finely and as eloquently as a poet laureate his love for her. With a flash of insight, she knew he'd needed this moment more than she, had needed to say these things more than she needed to hear them. No matter what her choice might be in the end.

Kenny's face revealed clearly that he hadn't expected this tack. He took a step forward, fists raised in a hysterical, last-ditch effort to save the situation, to save himself. To save Wayne. Nate's hands clenched at his sides, ready, for he would fight Kenny, just as he stated. And he'd win.

"No!" came the cry behind them.

They turned as one and saw Davey's stark face staring at them from behind the screen door. He'd obeyed Nate by staying inside, but Maura realized he'd been standing there all along and had heard every bit of the exchange between the two men.

"Oh, son," she whispered, her heart wrenching in agony for him.

The door crashed open as he hurled himself against it and stumbled onto the porch, but he stopped at the top step, his tortured gaze going from his mother to his uncle to Nate.

"N-no," he pleaded, his mouth working and tears trembling in his eyes. "Don't hurt him.... *Don't hurt my dad!*"

Time hung suspended, a moment and an eternity. Then Davey tore down the steps and across the yard toward the two men. As if paralyzed, they watched him come...to which of them?

It was Nate. Davey launched himself into his arms, holding on for dear life as Nate's eyes squeezed shut and he pressed his cheek hard against the bright head he held in his large hand.

Kenny stared at the two as his fists dropped slowly to his sides. His head swiveled to Maura, seeking...something. Anything. He looked lost. Lost as a child without a home.

Tears coursed down her cheeks, tears of relief and thankfulness. And compassion, as well—for Kenny. Whether anyone wanted to or not, the choice was made. And though she would have had it happen any other way than this, it had to be made.

Kenny saw that confirmation in her eyes, and he pivoted away, misery, but no longer denial, in every angular bone. He took a few faltering steps to the walnut tree and leaned one forearm against it, his hand splayed on its rough trunk. Head bent, he stood motionless for several minutes before his hand closed. Then he lifted his fist from the tree trunk, held, and let it fall again to the bark.

Davey had watched his uncle from the circle of Nate's arms. Now he slid down to stand on the ground, though he still hugged Nate's thigh.

In that wordless communication they had between them, he looked up at Nate, a question.

Nate squeezed his shoulder, an answer.

Davey walked to his uncle, hesitated, then slipped his hand into the one that hung at Kenny's side. An offer.

And after a moment, Kenny's fingers closed around the small ones in his palm.

An acceptance.

Maura turned and her gaze collided with Nate's. It took every ounce of her strength not to run to the circle of those strong arms also, but this was a turning point for the three men in her life; she wouldn't disrupt it. Besides, she had one very important task that remained.

She headed for the backyard, for her garden. There Maura sank slowly to her knees between the rows. Reaching out, she fingered a leaf, rubbing it gently between thumb and forefinger, drawing strength and solace and peace from these growing things as she always had and always would.

And she said goodbye to Wayne, too.

There were no words mumbled under her breath or spoken in her mind. From her heart it came, as a prayer would. She gave forgiveness—for dying. Then she waited, listening with her heart. And it came, no more than a wisp on the wind: She was forgiven—for living.

Two boots appeared next to her. Maura looked up into Nate's eyes.

He had his fingers crammed into his front jeans pockets, and his expression was remote, closed to emotion.

She frowned in puzzlement.

"Seems like I'm forever apologizing to you for something," he said, "but I want you to know I'm sorry about that scene out front, Maura. With Kenny."

"You needn't apologize for anything," she replied. "Under the circumstances, what else could you have done?"

"Sure beats me, but I know you never wanted to be in a position like that again, and—" He broke off, his gaze tearing away from hers as he restlessly scanned the horizon.

"I meant what I said," he pronounced abruptly. "It's unfortunate Davey got involved today, but I want you to know his trust isn't misplaced. Yours, either. You stuck up for my farming to the town, Maura, and I'll never forget that."

A quiver of apprehension went through her. It sounded as if *he* were saying goodbye. "I didn't do anything I wouldn't have—"

He held up a hand, clearly needing to speak his piece. "You defended my right to farm as I chose, and I just wanted you to know that, no matter what happens between us, you and Davey can count on me if you ever find yourself penned in again by whatever circumstances. You have a right to decide how to live your life and raise your son."

Then she understood. He didn't know—he couldn't know—that she had already decided.

"I see," she said, dropping her gaze to study her hands as they lay in her lap. "Well. I could use some advice right now, if you've got a minute."

The boots shifted. "Sure."

"I've been looking for something lately. Or perhaps I should say someone. A man, one who's faithful and hardworking—a farmer maybe?—and who loves little boys. Oh, and me. Someone I could love like . . . well, like a husband, but more," she whispered. "So much more. And I heard, Nate Farrell, that you're looking for a wife. Can you help me?"

A blackbird drifted down a wind current and brazenly lit on top of one of the bean poles. It cocked its head at both of them. The breeze it had come in on died suddenly, and the air became still.

What did they look like, she wondered, from the point of view of that beady black eye? Two ordinary people: a woman kneeling in her garden; a man, tall and straight. Not an unusual couple. Or would the blackbird discern the aura of love encircling and transforming them into more than just man and woman?

A large hand appeared before Maura's eyes, its palm callused from hard work, yet with long fingers that looked capable of incredible tenderness. She lifted her own hand and set it in Nate's. His fingers closed around it as he pulled her to her feet and into his arms. Wrapping her own arms around his waist, she pressed her cheek against his shoulder, absorbed the feel of his rough jaw against the crown of her head.

They stood like that for many a heartbeat, surrounded by each other's love, saying nothing but understanding everything as silent communication flowed between them.

Finally she lifted her head. His features were drawn. He looked like a man who'd been through hell and back. But what she saw in Nate's eyes was the same as she'd seen in Davey's, and she knew that it was the same as in her own—a wonder that what each of them so wanted was within their grasp at last.

"I love you, Nate, with all my heart."

"Maura, I—" His gaze roved over her face. He shook his head as his lips curved into a wry smile. "Words could never say what I feel for you."

He meant to show her, though, as his face bent to hers and they shared a kiss of commitment and love, fulfillment and promise.

Never had she felt so right, so completely in harmony, and Maura found herself amazed that she could be. But then she'd learned a powerful lesson: everything works together, but only if everything is pledged to that end.

She heard a flutter of wings, almost felt them brush her cheek as they passed. Maura opened her eyes just in time to see the blackbird disappear into the sky.

*   *   *   *   *

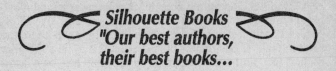

Silhouette Books
"Our best authors, their best books...

DIANA PALMER
Soldier of Fortune in February

ELIZABETH LOWELL
Dark Fire in February

LINDA LAEL MILLER
Ragged Rainbow in March

JOAN HOHL
California Copper in March

LINDA HOWARD
An Independent Wife in April

HEATHER GRAHAM POZZESSERE
Double Entendre in April

**When it comes to passion,
we wrote the book.**

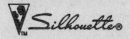

Take 4 bestselling love stories FREE

Plus get a FREE surprise gift!

Special Limited-time Offer

Mail to Silhouette Reader Service™

3010 Walden Avenue
P.O. Box 1867
Buffalo, N.Y. 14269-1867

YES! Please send me 4 free Silhouette Romance™ novels and my free surprise gift. Then send me 6 brand-new novels every month, which I will receive months before they appear in bookstores. Bill me at the low price of $2.19 each plus 25¢ delivery and applicable sales tax, if any.* That's the complete price and—compared to the cover prices of $2.75 each—quite a bargain! I understand that accepting the books and gift places me under no obligation ever to buy any books. I can always return a shipment and cancel at any time. Even if I never buy another book from Silhouette, the 4 free books and the surprise gift are mine to keep forever.

215 BPA ANRP

Name	(PLEASE PRINT)	
Address	Apt. No.	
City	State	Zip

This offer is limited to one order per household and not valid to present Silhouette Romance™ subscribers. *Terms and prices are subject to change without notice. Sales tax applicable in N.Y.

HE'S MORE THAN A MAN, HE'S ONE OF OUR

Fabulous Fathers

CALEB'S SON
by Laurie Paige

Handsome widower Caleb Remmick had a business to run and a son to raise—alone. Finding help wasn't easy—especially when the only one offering was Eden Sommers. Years ago he'd asked for her hand, but Eden refused to live with his workaholic ways. Now his son, Josh, needed someone, and Eden was the only woman he'd ever trust—and the only woman he'd ever loved....

Look for *Caleb's Son* by Laurie Paige, available in March.

Fall in love with our Fabulous Fathers!

Silhouette
ROMANCE™

FF394

It's our 1000th
Silhouette Romance
and we're celebrating!

Join us for a special collection of love stories by the authors you've
loved for years, and new favorites you've just discovered.

**It's a celebration just for you,
with wonderful books by
Diana Palmer, Suzanne Carey,
Tracy Sinclair, Marie Ferrarella,
Debbie Macomber, Laurie Paige,
Annette Broadrick, Elizabeth August
and MORE!**

Silhouette Romance...vibrant, fun and emotionally rich! Take another
look at us!

As part of the celebration, readers can receive a FREE gift AND enter
our exciting sweepstakes to win a grand prize of $1000! Look for
more details in all March Silhouette series titles.

**You'll fall in love all over again
with Silhouette Romance!**

And now for
something completely different
from Silhouette....

Unique and innovative stories that take you into the world of paranormal happenings. Look for our special "Spellbound" flash—and get ready for a truly exciting reading experience!

In February, look for
One Unbelievable Man (SR #993)
by Pat Montana.

Was he man or myth? Cass Kohlmann's mysterious traveling companion, Michael O'Shea, had her all confused. He'd suddenly appeared, claiming she was his destiny—determined to win her heart. But could levelheaded Cass learn to believe in fairy tales...before her fantasy man disappeared forever?

Don't miss the charming, sexy and utterly mysterious
Michael O'Shea in
ONE UNBELIEVABLE MAN.
Watch for him in February—only from

As seen on TV!
Free Gift Offer

With a Free Gift proof-of-purchase from any Silhouette® book,
you can receive a beautiful cubic zirconia pendant.

This gorgeous marquise-shaped stone is a genuine cubic
zirconia—accented by an 18" gold tone necklace.

(Approximate retail value $19.95)

Send for yours today...
compliments of ▼ *Silhouette*®

To receive your free gift, a cubic zirconia pendant, send us one original proof-of-purchase, photocopies not accepted, from the back of any Silhouette Romance™, Silhouette Desire®, Silhouette Special Edition®, Silhouette Intimate Moments® or Silhouette Shadows™ title for January, February or March 1994 at your favorite retail outlet, together with the Free Gift Certificate, plus a check or money order for $2.50 (do not send cash) to cover postage and handling, payable to Silhouette Free Gift Offer. We will send you the specified gift. Allow 6 to 8 weeks for delivery. Offer good until March 31st, 1994 or while quantities last. Offer valid in the U.S. and Canada only.

Free Gift Certificate

Name: _____

Address: _____

City: _____ State/Province: _____ Zip/Postal Code: _____

Mail this certificate, one proof-of-purchase and a check or money order for postage and handling to: SILHOUETTE FREE GIFT OFFER 1994. In the U.S.: 3010 Walden Avenue, P.O. Box 9057, Buffalo NY 14269-9057. In Canada: P.O. Box 622, Fort Erie, Ontario L2Z 5X3.

FREE GIFT OFFER   079-KBZ
ONE PROOF-OF-PURCHASE
To collect your fabulous FREE GIFT, a cubic zirconia pendant, you must include this
original proof-of-purchase for each gift with the properly completed Free Gift Certificate.

079-KBZ